I got pregn~~ant~~
father and ~~~~

And then fell in ~~~~
her heart aching. ~~~~
all was, as sharp ~~~~, named
and waiting for her ~~~~

She loved Tom Callahan, and she wanted him to feel that way about her. But how could he? The prenuptial agreement alone bore witness to their shared caution in their marriage of convenience. It contained forty-seven clauses!

But it said nothing about what had happened yesterday...and their overpowering physical hunger for each other...

After living in the USA for nearly eight years **Lilian Darcy** is back in her native Australia with her American historian husband and their three young children. More than ever, writing is a treat for her now, looked forward to and luxuriated in like a hot bath after a hard day. She likes to create modern heroes and heroines with good doses of zest and humour in their make-up.

Lilian Darcy also writes for Mills & Boon Medical Romance™.

THE SURROGATE
MOTHER

BY
LILIAN·DARCY

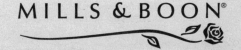

MILLS & BOON®

First published in Great Britain 2000
Harlequin Mills & Boon Limited,
Eton House, 18-24 Paradise Road, Richmond, Surrey TW9 1SR

© Melissa Benyon 1999

ISBN 0 263 82002 5

Set in Times Roman 10½ on 12¼ pt.
01-0007-40916

Printed and bound in Spain
by Litografía Rosés, S.A., Barcelona

Chapter One

This, at last, was Loretta's husband.

Julie had only a few seconds to marshal her first impressions of the man who had been married to her cousin. Tom Callahan was coming toward her across the polished hardwood floor of this spacious and blessedly cool office.

Her very soul ragged with fatigue and stress, she saw that he was tall, dark-haired, golden tanned, denim-clad and somewhere in his early thirties.

And then he had reached her, and taken her hot hands into his cool ones. They looked at each other for a moment, their hands locked together, not yet knowing what to say, how to begin.

Despite the awkwardness, the engulfing pressure of his touch was like a lifeline.

Then carefully, as a tribute to the circumstances

of this, their first meeting, he took her into his arms. It didn't seem odd. On Tuesday, also, at Loretta's sparsely attended funeral, Julie had found herself being hugged by strangers.

"Julie," he said eventually. His voice sounded deeper and huskier than it had on the phone yesterday.

"Tom," she managed to say.

He was strong, athletic. She could feel it in the hard, warm knots of muscle that filled out his upper arms and in the squared pectorals of his chest. She hadn't expected such a powerfully physical man. It helped a little. Physically, right now, she simply needed the support.

As well, she had begun to realize just how strongly every detail, every attribute of this man would live on in her future. Distractedly, she had already registered that he was one of the best looking men she'd ever met. Now, detail added to detail.

His eyes were as dark and glowing as polished teak. His thick hair was the color of molasses shafted by sunlight. Just a tad untidy and too long on top, it was hair that could make a woman want to reach out and smooth it into place with a caress.

In his arms, she closed her eyes, drew a waft of his mellow male scent into her nostrils and felt the shaking in her limbs, in contrast to his quiet steadiness. He must have felt it also. His arms tightened and he said her name again, with his lips against her hair. She felt the warmth of his breath and heard the thud of his heartbeat.

"It was good of you to come up." His voice resonated deep in his chest.

"I needed to," she told him.

It was truer than he could yet know. He *would* know by the end of their meeting today. On the journey by plane and car from Philadelphia, she'd thought of little else. Tom Callahan's part-time maintenance man, Don Jarvis, had brought her here from the Albany airport, and she'd barely managed to pass the time of day with the man. Fortunately, having given her his careful condolences about Loretta's death, Don probably hadn't expected much in the way of conversation.

Tom let her go at last, slowly, as if to make sure she had the strength to stand up. They stood facing each other, not touching any more but still standing close.

"This is hard," he said. She could see in the twist of his face how much he meant it.

"It has to be, doesn't it?" she agreed, her throat tight.

"I'm sorry I couldn't meet you at the airport myself."

"No, please! I asked you on the phone not to disrupt your schedule."

"You see, when you called yesterday, I—" He broke off and shook his head, unable to find words, then reached back to wipe a lean hand around the inside of his open collar. "Look," he began again after a moment, "I'm going to give my assistant, Marcia, the rest of the day off, then we'll talk. We need to give this some time, and we don't need interruptions from *anyone*. I'm so sorry you couldn't track me down before the funeral."

"Yes. So am I. I did try."

"I was on the west coast for a couple of days."

"And Loretta didn't seem to have this address and phone number written down anywhere obvious. I looked through her papers a little, but there was a lot of other stuff to do, and—"

"I know you did," Tom was saying. "And I appreciate it. This must have been a horrific few days for you. Just excuse me for a moment."

He went to the outer office, and Julie heard the low vibration of his voice as he gave his assistant some instructions.

It gave her time to think, and to feel once more the growing unease that had begun five days ago, just hours after she had learned of Loretta's death. Why had it taken her nearly four days to find any reference to Tom Callahan's summer address amongst Loretta's papers? He was her husband! Yet Tom himself had not seemed surprised that Julie couldn't track him down.

Something was very wrong. Something didn't gel.

Tired to the bone after five nights of shredded sleep, she sank into one of the two rust-brown leather armchairs facing the floor-length windows that overlooked Diamond Lake. The cool leather was as soft as cream. At once, the peace and beauty of the place started its healing work. Tom Callahan's summer retreat stood on its own private island, surrounded by a bright mirror of limpid water, with the folded, forested Adirondack mountains beyond. She understood exactly why he had chosen this place. What she didn't understand was—

He was back. He set a tray on the small table then pulled up the second armchair and sat down, his long thighs jutting from the leather seat.

He'd brought coffee. Two steaming mugs of it. Her stomach rebelled, but she craved something to do with her hands and something to fill her mouth, so she answered his questioning look with, "Yes, thanks. Lots of cream. And some sugar, too, please." Maybe the sweetness would keep back the nausea that had been rising in her all morning.

"Not watching your weight?" Tom teased carefully, adding a large dollop of cream to her mug.

"Not at the moment."

He was, though, Tom realized. Not watching her weight, but watching her body. She was beautiful, even handicapped by the fatigue and stress that had put slate-blue shadows beneath her blue eyes and tightened her long, graceful limbs.

Her wheat-blond hair was looped on her head so that a few tendrils fell in long, bouncy curves. He wanted to wind his fingers through them. Her skin was as smooth and warm-hued as ripe apricots, with just the airbrushed hint of dappled gold freckles across her nose. And she had the most incredibly warm, generous mouth he'd ever seen.

Tom shifted and sent a spoonful of sugar fanning across the tray. It didn't matter. The mess was nothing. It was all contained on the tray. He dug into the sugar bowl and got another, but the clumsy action disturbed him all the same.

He hadn't thought at all about what Loretta's cousin would be like. He definitely hadn't considered the possibility that he might find her in any way attractive. Perhaps the low, emotion-filled music of her voice on the phone yesterday, during their painfully clumsy conversation, should have told him something.

He didn't *want* to be attracted to her. He was a free man emotionally, and no one who knew him would question his right to that freedom, but he didn't want this difficult meeting to get any more complex than it had to be. For both of them, this was about endings, not beginnings. After today, it was doubtful they'd ever need to meet again.

He pushed his physical awareness of her aside, stirred the sugar into her coffee and handed it to her.

Determined to get to the painful heart of this as quickly as possible, he said, ''You told me it was a car accident. Was it quick? Was she at the wheel?''

''It was instantaneous, the police told me. For both of them. The car was traveling at over ninety miles an hour.''

"Both of them?" Tom queried automatically, though he wasn't really surprised. Not if he recalled all those times in the past when he'd thought Loretta was alone and she hadn't been.

Julie fisted a hand in front of her mouth and cleared her throat. She had no choice but to tell the truth. "There was someone else at the wheel," she said huskily. "A man."

The words tasted like cardboard. She had wanted to get all this over quickly, yes, but had expected a little more opportunity to prepare him...and herself. Small talk meant nothing at a time like this, but it had its uses. Tom Callahan, on the other hand, clearly preferred to look things in the face.

Her stomach twisted. A gulp of coffee didn't help. Made things worse, in fact.

This was Tom's wife they were talking about. Sure, the marriage had had problems. Loretta herself had admitted that. She'd talked about it in exhaustive, passionate detail. Their separation. Their attempts at reconciliation. The baby they'd both wanted—the baby that hadn't come, even after infertility treatment.

But despite all of this, Loretta was still Tom's wife, and as of last week there was every hope of the two of them successfully resuming their marriage. Or so Julie had believed up until last Sunday. Now, she was far from sure.

"His name was Phillip Quinn," she said, unable to blur the truth with tact. This was a truth you *couldn't* blur. "And according to his family, Tom, they were lovers. I'm...so sorry."

She forced herself to look at him, steeled against what she expected to find—the sight of despair and shock written in the dark good looks of his face. It was hard enough for *her* to contemplate—hell, it just didn't make *sense!* But for him...

Instinctively, she reached out to take his hand, and he let her, until she realized how she was chafing it, pulling the tanned skin back and forth across the well-shaped muscles and sinews. Then she practically dropped his hand onto the arm of the chair. In the background came the sound of Don Jarvis starting the motorboat again. She assumed he was taking Tom's assistant back to shore.

"I'm sorry, too," Tom said, his voice low and steady. "That two people should die that way. Ninety miles an hour! That's a heck of a speed to be traveling, and on city streets."

"But—" Her hands splayed convulsively.

"Did you think it would come as a shock?" he said quietly. "Did you think it would hurt me?"

"Your wife and another man? Of course I—"

"Julie, Loretta was unfaithful to me five years ago. More than once. That's why—partly why—we split up. Our divorce was a long way from being friendly, and it's been finalized for three years. I've seen her twice since, both times at her insistence, and both times it's been ugly. She was once a big part of my life, yes, and no one deserves to die that way and that young, but I can't bleed for Loretta now, and if she did have a lover and was happy with him in the moments before she died, then I'm glad for her. Maybe she *was* starting to accept it at last.''

Divorced. Tom and Loretta were actually *divorced?* And Julie knew that Loretta *hadn't* accepted it at all. The house, the whole earth seemed to rock, and Tom Callahan's face, with his teak dark eyes fixed so intently on Julie's expression, turned a pretty shade of golden yellow then faded altogether.

She felt him grab the hot coffee mug from her limp grip just in time, then she sank into the supportive depth of the chair. Her eyes were closed, her mind whirling.

She didn't for a moment doubt the truth of his words. They made far too much sense. Divorced for three years. It was why, in the pathological chaos of Loretta's apartment—the apartment Julie had assumed was Tom's Philadelphia home, as well—it had taken her so long to find a reference to his Diamond Lake phone number and address. It explained the sense of uneasiness she'd had as she began to sort through Loretta's things, and the mounting certainty that the whole situation was not as she'd believed it to be.

Loretta had lied. She'd lied big-time. To herself, perhaps, as much as to everyone else.

''A rocky patch,'' she had called it. ''A temporary separation. We both just needed space. But if I could give Tom a baby. He's always wanted kids, and I'm so ready to be a mom, Julie. So ready. My career at the cable station means nothing. I just want Tom, and his baby, and to be a family. I know it's what he wants, too.''

Pacing in her apartment, two months ago, like a caged animal.

''This infertility thing is killing us, Julie, and it's strangling our marriage. Slowly, like…like a pair of hands just gradually squeezing together, tighter and tighter. We both agreed it was best to take a break over the summer while I started looking for a surrogate mother. That's why Tom has gone to the lake. We worked out the contract before he left.

''We just couldn't stand what we were doing to each other, you see. We were both hurting so bad we'd just lash out over nothing, and then realize and cry and apologize and make promises and break them again two days later. The idea of sur-rogacy and the terms of the contract are about all we've agreed on in weeks. Taking a break is the right thing.''

Why had she lied like that? She had changed Ju-lie's whole life with those lies.

''Julie, are you all right?'' Tom's voice, dark and low, came out of the mist that enveloped her.

She struggled to open her eyes and banish the dizziness in her head. A couple of deep breaths brought control, but her stomach was turning over. The nausea again.

''You look terrible,'' he accused, concern etched onto his face.

"Yes… I'm pregnant." She waited for a reaction, every muscle and nerve ending coiled. She doubted what Loretta had told her on this issue, too. Perhaps Tom *did* know. But the loaded word didn't trigger a flash of understanding. Instead, it only deepened his look of concern.

And he didn't waste any time clucking in sympathy. "I'll get dry crackers and water," he said, already on his feet. "Salted potato chips, too. Don't move, okay? It'll take just a minute."

She tried to get up, to say something polite, but he'd already gone. She stayed where she was, fighting hard against the rebellion in her stomach. Over the past few days, it had gotten to be a more and more familiar feeling.

She wondered how Tom had been able to recognize the symptoms and prescribe the remedy so quickly. A week or two ago, Julie herself wouldn't have had any idea just how desperately a woman in the first trimester of pregnancy could need crackers and chips.

It had to be fatigue, as well, of course, that had made her nausea get so bad so fast. As Loretta's closest known relative—almost her *only* known relative—Julie had been the one to make all the arrangements, deal with the practicalities. No close friends of Loretta's had shown up with offers of assistance, either. Julie had worked alone from early morning until late at night for days.

There was more to do. Loretta's apartment was still in chaos. It would have been easier to have someone to share the task with, but Loretta's father had walked out years ago, and her mother—Julie's aunt Anne—had died when Julie was eighteen. Aunt Anne had outlived her brother, Jim, Julie's beloved father, by just five years. As for Julie's mother, Sharon, Loretta's aunt by marriage...

Well, Mom was very happy these days, so perhaps it wasn't fair that Julie felt totally brushed aside and unable to ask for help when she needed it. Mom's second husband was a thirty-seven-year-old would-be actor, still waiting for his big break, and Sharon Gregory was more obsessive than any stage mother in chasing opportunities for him.

She'd kept dad's last name when she remarried purely so she could describe herself as Matt Kady's agent without revealing a conflict of interest. And she seemed to hate the fact that Julie, at twenty-three, proved her old enough to have a grown child.

It was this new distance from her mother that had given Julie the final push she needed to leave California and return to Philadelphia, where she'd lived until the age of nine. And that, of course, was how she'd gotten close to Loretta again over the past three months, after they hadn't seen each other in more than thirteen years.

Gotten close? She was starting to doubt that now.

"Here."

Tom was back, with a huge glass of iced water, a freshly opened packet of saltine crackers and a package of chips. Strange chips. He apologized for

them at once, while Julie was chewing on her first
cracker, feeling the salt begin to settle her stomach.

"I'm sorry about these." He held up the packet.
"Unfortunately they're Bovril flavored." His expression was so full of pained regret that Julie almost laughed.

"What is Bovril?" she managed faintly, taking
them anyway. The saltines weren't quite salty
enough. Maybe the chips would settle the craving.

"It's this strange brown drink they have in En-
gland," Tom answered, playing the moment for all
it was worth. He could see that Julie badly needed
a break.

"Hot and sort of beefy," he went on. "I was
there on business last month and... Well, you see,
I have this running gag with my brother Liam. I'm
on a mission to find the world's most bizarre snack
foods for him to try." He grinned, as if he hoped
to coax a smile from her as well. "He's sixteen,
and comes up here from Philly a lot in summer."

"And what did he think of these?" Julie asked,
her attention caught now.

It felt almost as good to break their fraught conversation with this moment of lightness as it felt to
break her nausea with the crackers. He was doing
it deliberately, distracting her with nonsense and
she was deeply grateful for his perception.

"He hasn't tried them yet. He's working up to it
with the safer flavors," Tom explained, deadpan.
"So far he's tackled ketchup, roast turkey with stuff-
ing and pickled onions, if I remember correctly."

"Oh. Yummy. Pickled onions, huh?"

Yes! There it was! Tom thought. It didn't last long. Like a shaft of sunset light breaking through piled clouds and then fading, it was there for just a moment, but the effect of it practically knocked his socks off. Wide and radiant, lighting up her whole face, putting a tiny crease on either side of her pert little nose so that he noticed the freckles again and got a vivid image of her as a kid—a tomboy of a kid who caught frogs and climbed trees and whistled through her finger and thumb.

"To be honest," he admitted, still watching her, "they all taste mainly of salt."

"Really? Salt is what I want."

Julie picked up a cracker and took a bite. Her stomach and taste buds, much to her surprise, approved. She decided to take turns. Cracker. Chip. Water. Slowly.

Tom was watching her. Had been for a while, she knew. "You're having a hard time."

"Just these past few days."

"How far along are you?"

"Not far. About six weeks, the way doctors count it. Four weeks from when I, uh, conceived. I only took the test last Friday. Loretta…never knew."

"Early days, then," he said. His voice sounded a little strained at the mention of his ex-wife.

"Yes."

She gave a tight smile. Early days, and the cause of enormous upheaval in her life. A rethinking of everything in almost every waking moment for days. She was already deeply attached to the life that grew inside her. That didn't make sense, the way things had started out, but it had happened. She knew that she'd become a part of something important, something that mattered more than anything else, and if Tom could not respond to that and give her what she wanted...

"The nausea doesn't matter," she told him firmly. "This baby is the most important thing in the world to me, right now."

She managed to disguise the unnamed threat in her words, and he responded at once.

"That's great," he said. His face softened. "Babies are such incredible packages of hope and love and potential, aren't they? I'm really happy for you, Julie."

"Mmm." She dared to smile at him. He understood. It gave her a warm surge of hope. They could work something out, pull the right solution out of this mess.

Then his gaze flicked to her ringless left hand. His smile gave way to a tiny frown, and her stomach churned again. No, she wasn't married. She didn't even have a boyfriend. He'd know why soon enough.

"Hey." He'd seen that she was struggling again. He was bending down, coaxing her to her feet. "Is this okay? I'd like to get you outside for some fresh air. I had my housekeeper leave us lunch. I can bring it out to the balcony. There's a breeze off the water, and it's shady and cool.''

"That sounds great.''

He sounded great. So tender, and so concerned. To have someone care about her physical well-being was so unexpected and so wonderful that it threatened to completely break down the nervous tension, which was all that had kept her going since Sunday. She'd been feeling so alone!

He was holding her from behind, his hand curved like a warm velvet cuff around her forearm. The soft chambray of his shirt covered her bare arm. She could feel the heat of his body against her back through the fine fabric of her cream blouse, and for a moment she let herself sway back, surrendering her weight to his support.

For the first time she fully understood the meaning and significance of the child that grew inside her.

Cradling her in the curve of his arm as he led her through the house, Tom felt his unwanted attraction to her surge again. So she was pregnant! It made sense of the way she looked. There was a secret source to her beauty, which couldn't quite be explained by adding up her features and assets, since it came from deeper inside her. He felt the swollen fullness of one breast against the crook of his arm and knew that soon she would look as ripe as some lavish tropical fruit.

He wondered why she wasn't married and why she hadn't even mentioned a man.

A moment later, she retched, pressed her fist to her mouth and fought hard for control.

"Easy, easy," he soothed her, as if talking to a nervous colt. "Just take it slowly and keep hold of those crackers!"

"You seem to know…" she paused and chewed desperately, "a lot about this!" Julie got the words out safely.

"So I should," he answered her. "I've got six younger brothers. I spent months of my childhood on cracker patrol."

"*Six?*" She knew at once that Tom's mother must be more heroic than any warrior.

"And one who's older."

"And no girls?"

"No girls," he agreed cheerfully. "After about number four Mom stopped minding. She figured she and Dad just didn't have the chemistry in that department, and what the heck, she liked boys anyway."

"I like boys, too," she said. "I just about *was* one, as a kid. A classic tomboy, that is."

"Yeah, I thought you might have been," he muttered under his breath.

They reached the balcony. Julie hadn't taken much notice of the route. Mostly, she'd been looking hard at the floor. Hardwood in some places, slate in others. A couple of large, expensive squares of Turkish carpet. Somehow, she hadn't guessed that he would be quite so well off and so obviously successful.

Now, Tom settled her in a slat-backed wooden patio chair and promised, "I'll be back with lunch, okay?"

"Okay," she nodded.

He was right. It felt a lot better out here in the open.

This balcony didn't face the dock where she'd arrived. Instead, the light dazzled on the water just beyond a crescent of sandy beach and a shelf of vibrant green lawn, edged with colorful plantings of annuals. A cool breeze blew, combing away the heavy heat, teasing her with its fresh breath on her forehead and cheeks.

Tom was back a few minutes later with turkey club sandwiches crammed with filling, plain iced soda water and a huge bunch of sweet green grapes.

"Mom lived on these, too, I seem to recall." He grinned.

"I'll try one."

Julie pulled a grape off its stem and bit down on the taut, satiny skin. At once it burst in her mouth, and she tasted the flood of sweet juice. Heaven! He gave a grin of sympathy and took a bite of sandwich, revealing teeth that were even, pearl-sheened and perfect.

Then suddenly, now that they were settled, the tension was in the air again. They ate in silence for several minutes before Tom spoke at last. "You seemed shocked to hear that Loretta and I were divorced," he said. "Was she spinning you a line about us planning to get back together?"

"Yes." Julie wasn't surprised that he had zeroed right to what concerned them both. There seemed no point in softening the reply.

"How well did you two know each other?" It sounded like an accusation. "How close were you?"

"She saved my life when I was nine."

And it made her sterile, although neither of us knew that then.

"That's close," he agreed slowly.

"It is. Or it was. And I've felt that debt to her, felt my gratitude to her ever since, even during the years we didn't see each other," Julie said, then found herself telling the story as if she'd known Tom for weeks instead of less than an hour.

"She was sixteen when it happened. Our families were vacationing together at a small ski resort in Vermont. We'd rented a little cabin. Nothing luxurious. We were skating one evening, and I fell. A kid came past and ran right over my left arm with a hockey skate. It tore open an artery—I still have the scar—and about ten minutes later, the big storm they'd been forecasting came down with a bang. They couldn't get me farther than the little local hospital.

"Nothing could fly in, either. The airport and helipad were both closed for more than forty-eight hours. I'd lost a lot of blood, and they were out of a match for my type. Out of O negative, also, which anyone can take safely. Loretta's blood was the only match they could find in a hurry. She gave me two pints, one that night and one the next morning. More than was really safe for her, but only just enough to pull me through.

"Two days later she came down with toxic shock syndrome. In all the drama, she'd forgotten she was finishing her period. She got to be more ill than I was, far more ill, Tom. You know what happened to her. You know how badly her tubes and ovaries were scarred."

"Yes." He nodded, his face tight. "The doctors told us that was what made it impossible for her to conceive. I didn't realize, though, that you were involved."

"Involved? It was my *fault*." Her voice rose.

"No." He shook his head urgently. "That's way too extreme, Julie."

"If I'd known…. If my parents had known what it would ultimately cost her to give me that blood…"

"But you didn't know. How could you?"

"And yet Loretta never once said to me, 'It's your fault.'"

"Yes," Tom agreed quietly. "She did have moments of surprising heroism sometimes."

"She seemed like a heroine to me then, when I was nine. She told me a couple of months ago that she'd gotten a kick out of the drama—"

"Yes, I can imagine that." He gave a faint, crooked smile.

"But that doesn't take away from what she did and what it cost her!" she said angrily.

Tom's hostility towards his ex-wife was coming through loud and clear, and blood was thicker than water. Just exactly *why* had Loretta been so desperate that she would lie about the state of her marriage to Tom, anyway? Suddenly, Julie distrusted him.

"She wasn't spinning me a line," she told Tom hotly. "She may have lied about your divorce, but she *did* want you back! You said so yourself."

"Not exactly. But we'll let that pass. She wanted me back so badly that she'd taken a lover in order to forget me, is that it?" he questioned.

His reasoning floored her. Yes, how *could* Loretta have gotten involved with another man at such a time? But she ignored it and attacked.

"So badly that she was prepared to have another woman bear a baby for her just to make you a father. I don't know what the truth is about your marriage or your divorce, Tom Callahan, but this baby I'm carrying is yours!"

Chapter Two

Telling him in anger was the worst way possible. Julie hadn't intended to do it that way. After all, she wanted him to *understand*. It was a bombshell of an announcement to make out of the blue, since she had evidence mounting every minute that he knew nothing about any of this. She could hardly condemn his white-hot reaction.

"That's... That's... Damn it to hell, what *is* this?" Tom sprang to his feet and began to prowl the balcony, then spun on his heel to face her. She had lightning flashing in her blue eyes, but he was angrier, and his first thunderstruck reaction was plain, old-fashioned disbelief. "Some kind of *scam* you've cooked up between you?" he accused. It was the only thing he could think of that could make sense.

"Scam?" she shrieked.

"There's only one reason Loretta wanted us to get back together, Julie," he told her bluntly. "And that's because after she left me five years ago—with another man, and not the first, either, although I didn't know *that* at the time—the business my brother Pat and I had been putting our guts into for years finally began to pay off. We made millions within a year of Loretta's and my separation. She kicked herself from that moment on for not hanging in there a bit longer. She wanted my money, that's what she wanted, and the baby—if there *is* a baby! I mean, *hell*, how can there be? The idea of the baby was just her last-ditch attempt to get her hands on my spending power."

"What do you mean 'if' there's a baby? You can't be suggesting I'd make this up! Make up something like this? Our child? Growing inside me?"

They glared at each other. It seemed impossible to Julie that this was the same man who'd cosseted her nausea so tenderly and capably just minutes earlier. And yet... And yet...

"Just tell me, Julie," he said quietly, holding his hands away from his sides like a Dodge City sheriff about to go for his guns, "Just tell me." He raked her with his dark eyes. "You came back to Philly a few months ago, right?"

"That's right."

"You were getting to know Loretta again. And since her death you've been going through her things, sorting out her life. You said yourself she was killed in her lover's car. She told you we were just recently separated, but I can show you a copy of our divorce decree, and it's three years old. From what you've come to know of her, do you really take everything she told you at face value now?''

"No, I don't," Julie retorted. "You're right. What she told me is as full of holes as a piece of Swiss cheese, but she's not me, okay? I'm for real. It took me a lot of soul-searching to agree to what she wanted, although, heaven knows, I owed it to her after what the consequences of my accident had done to her body. And I made *her* think about it, too. I told her to *really think* about whether she wanted to have a baby this way, and she convinced me she did.

"I didn't conceive this child to come into the world unwanted. I could never have done that! When I went to that clinic in Philly and conceived a baby with my egg and your sperm, I was acting in the belief that I was creating a being who'd fulfill the dearest wish of two people who, at heart, loved each other and were meant to be together.

"I've read enough about infertility to know how it can rip loving couples apart. From every word Loretta said, I believed I'd be nurturing a baby who'd make something *right* between the two of you, so that when I gave it up to you and Loretta after birth, it would be a blessing for all of us. That was the *only* way I'd have done it, and now to hear you talking about a *scam!*

"Like it or not, this baby is yours, Tom. Yours and mine, and most of why I've come up here today is so we can talk about what we're going to do about it!"

"You mean you want to get rid of it?" he demanded.

"*No!* That's the last thing in the world I'd ever consider. Damn you, why are you suddenly treating me like a—"

"Sorry. I'm sorry," he interrupted urgently. He'd flashed out in anger, but with the small part of his rational brain that was still in control he knew that conflict wasn't going to help. "But this has hit me like a ton of bricks." He was fighting to make her understand. "I knew nothing about it, okay?"

"But I have the surrogacy contract in my bag." Her hands were curled around the edge of the table so tight that her knuckles were white. "It has your signature on it, and it's dated this past April. Less than three months ago. Loretta said that you both agreed on it before you came up here, and that you'd agreed she'd spend the summer finding a mother. And at the clinic, too, there was a frozen batch of your— You *must* have agreed for artificial insemination to—"

"Yes," he said. "Five and a half years ago, when we were pursuing our options, my semen was banked there. Not three months ago. Someone was bribed, Julie, and my signature on that surrogacy contract of Loretta's was forged. I *didn't* give my permission for anything like this!"

Julie was shaking. Shaking so hard that Tom saw it and couldn't stand it. "Hey, hey…" he said, and tried to take her in his arms again.

A baby. *Their* baby. And yet, until an hour ago, they'd never met. It was…earth-shattering.

"Let me go, Tom." She meant it, too. She was fighting him off.

"Sure you're okay?"

"Yes. And we need to talk this out." She splayed her fingers onto the table for support, battled to gather her thoughts, then straightened and said, "First, I'm going to keep the baby. There's no question of that. That's got to be the ground rule in whatever we work out!"

She lifted her chin and her blue eyes glittered, as if she was daring him to question the statement. He did, too. This was too important to take at face value. "What will a baby do to your life?" he said.

She wasn't fazed. "What it does to any single mother's life, I expect. It'll change my plans, change my priorities, change my finances. Change everything."

It could have sounded too blunt and too cold, except that he saw the way her hands had come to curve around her stomach. She wasn't even aware of the gesture, but he understood it. She was already protecting the child, thinking of its well-being.

"Okay," he said a little more gently, biding his time. "And are there any more of these ground rules of yours?"

She sighed shakily. "That I don't know, Tom.

You tell me. There's the surrogacy contract. The most important reason I came up here today was to persuade you to tear it up. But since you're telling me that Loretta forged it in the first place and you knew nothing about it, I guess that's not going to be a problem?''

Not a problem? Tom rebelled violently, but said nothing.

"Loretta had led me to believe that you'd be ecstatic about becoming a father. I thought I might have had a fight on my hands. But obviously that's not going to be the case. I'm glad,'' she admitted, and her face twisted a little. "I might as well tell you, a fight over an issue like this is something I wasn't looking forward to!''

Again, he rebelled. She was acting as if his part in this was over and as if all the decisions were hers. That wasn't true, not by a long shot! An awareness of what *he* wanted, what was right for *him,* began to crystallize inside him. He might have had no inkling of its conception, but this was his child, too!

"No!'' he told her. "Absolutely *not!*'' She gasped, and he said bluntly, "Don't make the mistake of thinking anything is resolved, Julie. You're assuming that because I knew nothing about the baby before, I don't want anything to do with it now. But that's not true. I want this baby in my life. I want it very much!''

Tom sat on the balcony watching the shadows lengthen and the light begin to change across the lake. In his left hand, he cradled a glass in which the level of whiskey was sinking far too fast.

He lifted the glass to his lips and took a tiny sip, determined to nurse the drink as long as he could. He really needed to think.

He'd told Julie so, and she'd agreed that they both needed space. She was looking so drained he suggested she lie down in one of the spare bedrooms his housekeeper kept ready for family visits. If she'd been any less exhausted, she might have argued, but she was practically dropping in her tracks by the time he got her upstairs.

That was nearly an hour ago, and he hadn't heard a sound from her. He hoped she was fast asleep. Pregnant women needed it.

And pregnant women who'd been through what she had this past week probably needed it in triplicate.

Tom felt torn in two. The knowledge that he had fathered a child, albeit unknowingly and through medical technology, was pulling at the most primitive part of his maleness. He felt virile, earthy and powerfully potent. Complementing this was an instinctive need to nurture and protect and provide for.

And yet, on some level, he still didn't quite trust Julie. She was Loretta's cousin, after all.

Loretta.

He'd assumed Julie wanted to see him out of a need for closure, and he'd welcomed her for that reason. He needed closure himself on the subject of his ex-wife's life and death. After all, they'd been married for nine years. But closure wasn't going to be easy now. Loretta had left a typical legacy—one of drama and mess and a huge potential for ongoing conflict.

Yet Loretta Nash Callahan had never been an evil person. Her father's callous abandonment of his wife and child when Loretta was deep into the hormonal turmoil of adolescence had left its mark, as had the financial struggle that followed.

Attractive and ambitious, Loretta had snared a job as an anchor on a rather tacky local cable TV station at the age of twenty-one. But it had never led to more glamorous work with a major network, as she'd hoped, despite the fact that, as he learned afterward, she'd slept with *all* the right people.

If motherhood had come, perhaps her stalled career would have mattered less. Perhaps there'd have been no affairs.

But Tom wasn't convinced of this. Loretta always had a problem with her priorities. And her principles.

Was Julie Gregory cut from the same cloth? he wondered. Did she have the scent of his money in her nostrils? A seasoned campaigner would have no trouble collecting big time in this situation.

Tom knew that, if it came to the crunch, he'd pay for the baby if he had to. Pay to be allowed to give it the sense of well-being and belonging and permanent, rock-solid love he knew in his heart was so important.

He thought of his brother Adam, who'd gotten embroiled in a bad relationship last year and had a child now. A baby daughter, after all those Callahan boys. And poor Adam didn't have a clue where the baby or the mother had got to. They'd skipped town without a word. It was an ongoing source of pain to him and to the whole Callahan family, particularly Mom and Dad, who ached for their lost first grandchild, just a few months old.

Tom knew he'd pay Julie whatever she asked if she threatened something like that. He'd support her in luxury for the rest of her life.

"No!" he said. "She's not like that!"

Someone who smiled like a cute tomboy of a kid, someone who wrapped her hands around her belly to protect *his* baby…

He began to prowl, thinking of the woman who was carrying his child. The woman he'd met for the first time just hours ago. There was something about her. Was it her looks? She was pretty, beautiful, even, but her looks weren't model-perfect as Loretta's had been. And looks said nothing about character.

What was it that made him want to trust her, then, despite the deliberate cynicism the business world had bred in him over the years? It had to be more than her effect on his senses, didn't it?

He wasn't sure. Given a situation like this, how could anyone trust their own judgment?

"But you do, Tom," he told himself. "Against all good sense, there's something about her, and you trust her. So accept that, and go with it, and work out what you want."

That wasn't hard. *I want the baby. I want him in my life from the beginning, from now on, and I want to know that I'm not ever going to lose him.*

Or her. He didn't mind either way.

And insistently, no matter what options he played out in his mind, there was only one solution that really satisfied him. A bold, make-or-break solution that he'd be crazy to suggest and she'd be crazy to agree to. After another three hours of wrestling with the question, and his whiskey long gone, he knew he was going to suggest it anyway.

Someone was shaking Julie gently. Swimming out of deep sleep, she was totally disoriented. When she dragged her heavy lids open, she found that most of the light had gone from the unfamiliar room. All she could see was the shadowed bulk of a man's head and shoulders inches from her. A pair of liquid brown eyes glinted beneath impossibly thick lashes.

Tom Callahan.

At once, Julie was fully awake.

Then she realized something else. She wasn't dressed.

Julie scrambled into a sitting position then dived off the bed in search of her blouse. "If you'll leave now," she whispered, "I'll get dressed and be down in a minute."

"Fine," Tom agreed, his voice careful. "Barbara, my housekeeper, left a casserole this morning, and I've heated it up. We can talk over our options while we eat."

He got himself out of the room with almost indecent haste. His groin ached. On entering the dim twilight of the room to waken her, he hadn't seen that she was undressed. Since six he'd been wondering about rousing her, and had finally set a deadline for nine. He was impatient. They needed to talk.

But at nine, he'd found her still so deeply asleep that she hadn't stirred at the sound of his voice, so he'd instinctively knelt by the bed and reached for her shoulder. Only when skin touched skin had he realized she was wearing a silk spaghetti-strapped slip and very little else.

Even then, it had taken some seconds for his eyes to adjust to the lack of light and to then take in just how much of her he could see. She had such gorgeous skin, satin smooth and tanned pale gold. There were some more of those tiny tomboy freckles on her shoulders, too.

And her legs! He'd been astounded to realize how long they were now that he could see all the way up.

All the way up, to the most delicious little piece of female rear end he'd ever seen in his life. It was covered only by a pert triangle of satin and lace, because her silk slip had ridden up, and the way it had twisted around her showed off the sleekly curved tuck of her waist. Her pregnancy wasn't showing yet.

Correction. Her pregnancy wasn't showing at her *waist.*

His gaze had moved farther up and come to a screeching halt at two pouting swollen breasts, barely contained inside a saucy wisp of cream lace beneath the loose silk of her slip. It would have been a distinctly sexy bra even when she'd bought it, but still he was quite sure that back then it hadn't looked anywhere near so low-cut as it did now.

Quickly, he had turned his attention to her face and had to fight back a gush of breath. In sleep, and after six hours of nourishing rest, she looked like a dream come true.

Still shoeless, Julie heard him go. In a few seconds she could slip into her heeled pumps and catch up to him, but instead she stalled, needing more time to shake off the heaviness of sleep.

This high-ceilinged room was perched dramatically near the top of the house, with two huge windows that met at one corner to give the illusion that there was no wall between inside and out. The large, clear skylight added to the impression of space and nearness to nature. The room was simply furnished, in plain yet rich colors that offset the pale gold of the wood and the ancient, jewel-like patterns of a vibrant Turkish carpet.

Julie had trained in interior design and had just finished a three-month contract with one of Philadelphia's most prestigious firms of architects, yet she itched to take notes about the look and feel of Tom's vacation home. She knew he'd had a large hand in designing it.

Tom's house reminded her that she hadn't chosen interior design as a career because she wanted to gussy up corporate boardrooms, as she'd done at Case Renfrew.

She'd chosen it because she wanted to make *homes* for people. She wanted to make a place that *worked* for her clients, a place that reflected the best of who they were, the way Tom had made sure his house reflected him.

She wondered whether he was the hands-on type with everything, then realized with a shock of feeling that she knew the answer to this question already.

"I want the baby very much," he had said, and she hadn't understood until this moment how much that meant to her, what strength those words had given her.

She'd come up here this morning knowing almost nothing about him, too storm-tossed emotionally to begin to guess his reaction. She'd been terrified that he'd demand she hand the baby over entirely to him without a backward glance.

And then had come the shock of learning that Tom and Loretta were long divorced and he knew nothing about the surrogacy agreement. In that situation, she knew that many men would have treated her pregnancy as a disaster they wanted nothing to do with, something they'd *pay* to make go away.

Tom hadn't. He'd taken both copies of the surrogacy agreement from her and calmly fed them into Marcia Snow's sharp-toothed paper shredder.

But he didn't shred me, *my feelings.*

He wanted the baby. He wanted to be involved.

Knowing this made Julie feel less alone than she'd been since before her father's death almost ten years ago. She and Tom had said some harsh things to each other this afternoon. Thinking back, however, she didn't hold anything against him and hoped he felt the same about her.

For pity's sake, how could something like this *not* spark anger and hostility at some point? She felt none of that now.

Refreshed, wide awake, her nausea really gone for the first time in days, eager to hear what Tom had to suggest, Julie donned her shoes and went downstairs.

Julie gasped when she saw what Nick had done. The room, and the scene, looked perfect.

And the six-hour break had done something to the emotions of both of them. Peacefulness, respect, acceptance. *They were having a baby.*

It was getting dark, and the landscape outside was slowly mellowing to a blue velvet softness in which air and mountains and water become indistinguishable from each other. The large, airy house was very quiet—so quiet that a creak and a crack could be heard every now and then as the roof and external walls cooled after the hot summer day.

Nick touched a couple of switches to bring up golden pools of light, and then gestured at the laden table. ''Let's talk while we eat.''

As restless as a big cat while waiting for Julie to awaken, Tom had already set the food on the table, along with white wine for himself and a choice of juice or iced water for Julie, freshly poured into stemmed glasses. There were two tall red candles burning, and he'd found some flowers Barbara had arranged on the hall table and brought them in as a centerpiece—a small piece of craziness that fitted with the larger craziness to come.

If you were about to suggest to a near stranger that she hold your hand and leap with you off a sheer cliff of unknown height in pitch darkness, then you might as well set the scene in an appropriate manner.

He slid a chair back for Julie, and she sat opposite his place setting, close enough to touch him, wondering about the courtliness of his action. Was he simply safe-guarding the vessel that was carrying his child? It didn't seem that way. The gesture had been fluid and natural, suggesting that courtesy came naturally to him.

He sat, then slid the casserole and rice to her, and she ladled them onto her plate gratefully. Hunger had made her stomach start acting up again. This looked and smelled hot and delicious. And salty.

Tom wasn't saying much yet, but there was something very significant about being here with him like this, about to share a meal. Gradually, they were starting to build a relationship. It had to be that way. For better or worse, *they were having a baby*.

Tom's next words, however, shattered any illusory sense of calm Julie might have been feeling. ''I've thought about this now, and I know what I want,'' he said.

He leaned his strong forearms onto the table. He'd rolled his sleeves to the elbow, as if about to get down to a tough physical job. There was strength and confidence to him, and he didn't hesitate. His liquid voice contained all the authority of a businessman about to propose a merger…and perhaps that's exactly what it was.

''There's really only one answer. I want us to get married, Julie,'' he said. ''As soon as possible.''

Chapter Three

"Married!"

She'd expected all sorts of things, but not that. She'd been planning to agree to it all, too. A written acknowledgment that he was the father of the child? Sure! A contract stipulating partial custody on vacations and weekends? No problem! A shared say on issues such as schooling and TV privileges and dating? Why not! And if he'd proposed that the baby be ritually baptized at the age of eight months in a fire-walking ceremony performed by New Guinea highland tribesmen, she'd probably have given that idea respectful consideration, as well.

But *marriage?*

"That's insane!"

"Is it?"

"Yes. You can't be serious," she stated.

"But I am. Absolutely."

"That's—"

"Consider the other options," he urged. "*I* have. For hours. And however *we* might feel about them, we don't have the right to put ourselves first in this situation. We have to think of the baby."

"I *am* thinking of the baby!"

"Are you?" he demanded. "Let's see." He raised a long, tanned finger. "Number one, there's abortion." The word sounded blunt and ugly. "That sure as hell isn't thinking of the—"

"Agreed," she said sharply. "And I've already told you, that's *not* an option!"

"So delete that. Number two, I thank you very politely for coming, and for your interesting news, and wish you a nice life. Our child then grows up with a test tube for a father."

"You're making it sound—"

"I'm not going to lie to myself, Julie. Fathers matter. I should know. I've got a very good one, and the thought of my child growing up without that is—"

"Okay." She put down the fork she'd distractedly picked up. Food was suddenly irrelevant. "I've already said you can have as much input as you want."

"Input?" His mimicry rejected the word out of hand. "That's not enough."

"Until a few hours ago, you knew nothing about this."

"Until a few days ago," he retorted, "you were going to give the baby away."

"To my cousin, who'd lost the chance to bear her own children because of me. And to a loving couple, I thought."

"Well, okay, and now everything is different, and you've got all sorts of new feelings. Isn't that true?"

"Yes. Yes, of course, it is."

"Well, so have I."

Her voice was foggy. "I love this baby. The baby's not to blame for this mess."

"I'll be damned if I'm going to father a child and then lose it. Heaven knows, Loretta and I tried for four years to have a baby one way or another. I wanted kids. I still want them. But more importantly— Look!"

He dragged an old brown leather wallet from the back pocket of his jeans and flipped it open, then threw it across the table to Julie. It was a family photo. A *big* family. Tom's family. Him and those seven brothers he'd talked about, and their parents.

In the center was a dark-haired woman, a little faded, a little tired, a little soft and spreading around the middle but glowing in her happiness. Just behind her shoulder stood a man in his early fifties, graying at the temples and slightly stoop-shouldered.

Surrounding them were the boys. Julie had to count carefully. Yes, eight of them, ranging in age from maybe eight to around twenty-five, which meant that the picture must have been taken about eight years ago. And every one of the boys could have been Tom. All of them looked astonishingly alike—strong and dark and good-looking.

She picked him out eventually.

He and one of his brothers had been caught in the midst of a playful tussle. They had their arms locked in combat and grins on their faces that could never have been faked. White teeth, bright eyes, untidy hair, necks stretched, biceps bunched and jaws thrust out. The bond between them was totally apparent.

It was there in the rest of the group, as well, and Julie thought that she'd never seen a photo that spoke the word "love" more plainly. With no logic, only an overwhelming gut response, she suddenly wanted to be in that photo as well, to have her own cherished place in a family like that. It might make up, in part, for the loss of her father too soon, and for her mother's careless disappearance into a new life.

But what was she thinking? A phony marriage to Tom wouldn't make her part of his family.

"Eight of us kids," he said softly, persuasively. "Loved and wanted and protected and believed in."

"You all look alike," she said feebly.

"I know. That's genetics for you. No one could doubt we were brothers. No one could doubt who our parents were. I grew up with that—that sense of belonging and of knowing who I was. I'm not saying it can be or has to be like that for everyone, but I had it, and I want it for my child, and I *won't* settle for less, no matter what the circumstances!''

''You can't possibly mean that you think we should *stay* married!'' Julie said.

''Well, it's…highly unlikely, isn't it?''

For a telling moment, their eyes locked, then both looked quickly away. If the first step toward marriage was physical attraction then that, Julie realized with a shock, was certainly there.

It vibrated between them like an electric current, and yet, she hadn't fully recognized what it was until now. With all the other reasons for emotion between them, this was hardly surprising. In fact, the physical thing was probably the result of their emotions, more than anything else, she told herself. Like the proposed marriage, it wasn't real.

''But why not just—'' she began helplessly, fighting the idea like a fish caught in a net.

''Look.'' He fixed her with his dark gaze. ''Sure, there are different ways we could play this. But I want more than a weekend visitation every now and then. I want joint custody and full legal recognition of my status as this child's father.''

His eyes swept to her stomach, still flat and tidy beneath her flowered skirt.

''More than that, I want him, her, in my life,'' he went on. ''To love and know and grow with. And as part of my extended family. Permanently. To that end, I want marriage, and sharing a home, at least until the baby is born. For one thing, pregnancy can be tough. A woman needs support from *somewhere.* Why not take it from me?''

She laughed, a helpless sort of sound. It was all she could do. This whole thing was—

''You're right,'' he said softly, watching her. ''It *is* insane, isn't it? But then, this whole thing is insane. This whole situation. Did either of us wake up one morning and think to ourselves, 'Gee, one day I think I'd like to conceive a child with someone I've never met. Hell, you went into this out of a feeling that you wanted to help a blood relative who'd once helped you at great cost to herself, but you didn't know she was lying to you from the very beginning. That alone rocks the whole foundation of what you've done, wipes the slate clean.

''As for me, a few hours ago I'd have said I wasn't sure that I'd ever be a father, with the way things had worked out. And I sure wasn't planning on getting married again in the state of adolescent hormonal excitement I was in when I married Loretta. I was twenty then, and she was eighteen! If what we felt was love, then it's not a condition I hope to be in again.''

''And yet you're suggesting marriage to me.'' She meant it as a clever retort, a clinching argument against his crazy proposition, but he didn't treat it that way.

''You know what?'' he said thoughtfully. ''I really think maybe it's better this way. No expectations. No deceptive feelings. Just a commitment to respect each other and try as hard as we can. And a commitment to the baby.''

"Then you are thinking that this might last?"

"Stranger things have happened. Let's give it till the baby's born. A marriage of convenience, it's called, isn't it? No sex, and separate bank accounts, but we share everything else. We'll put it in writing, a prenuptial agreement, and after the baby comes, we'll renegotiate."

She was silent. He was serious.

"Hang on," he added. "I mean, of course, if you're involved with someone else—"

"No," she said. Too quickly. Another reason for leaving California three months ago.

Breaking up with Rick Lewis had been the right thing to do, but it hadn't been pleasant. Rick hadn't seen the need for the breakup. So what if he was sleeping with his secretary, as well? Julie had been of a distinctly different opinion on that point.

It was history now, but it had left its scar. On the whole, she shared more of Tom's cynicism on the subject of starry-eyed young love than she was prepared to admit. The question was, did she share his belief that a marriage based on the things *he'd* talked about had a chance of lasting more than a month?

"I need to think," she told him bluntly.

"I know," he agreed. "So let's eat. And afterward I'll take you to your motel. Unless you'd prefer to stay here."

"No," she answered quickly. "Thanks. But I need the break."

"Take it, then. I'm not pushing you into an answer on this. Not tonight."

The lake surface surrounding Tom's small Riviera powerboat was like black glass, and the cooling night was fresh. As they sped off, Julie let her hand fall and trail in the water, loving the thick, cold swim of it against her fingers, loving the exhilaration of speed.

Along the lakefront, there was an aura of peace and sleep. Vacationing families were heading for bed. It was almost midnight, and Tom was taking her to Bolton Landing where she'd made a motel reservation.

They were both drained by this time, and their silence came from a shared understanding that they'd had talked far too much today. But they'd surprised each other over the meal. There was no return to the edgy and at times explosive hostility of this afternoon. Instead, they'd talked of neutral things. Her work. His software company. The summer weather. His plans for landscaping the island, with Don's help. And at times they'd stayed silent, which was nicest of all.

As soon as they'd finished eating, he'd made the move to bring her ashore. She could have stayed in his house tonight. He'd issued the invitation once more, but she had to get away, and he had understood that.

Neutral territory. Time to consider and reflect.

Ten minutes later they were at the door of her motel—not quite the cheapest one in town, but close. She saw his skeptical glance at the chocolate brown and lemon yellow painted clapboard. The place was about as stylish as a Boy Scout camp, a deliberate economy on her part. With a baby to pay for, and not knowing what Tom's attitude would be, she'd been planning to save every cent she could.

He looked at her, his eyes narrowed and searching. He said softly, "You could have played this whole thing very differently, you know, Julie."

"*Played* it?"

"You could have asked for money. Quite a lot of money. I'm…kind of surprised you didn't."

He caught her wrist just in time to forestall the stinging slap she aimed at his tanned cheek.

"Hey, hey," he soothed. "Hell, I didn't mean it that way!" he persisted urgently. "I *didn't!* Look, I put it badly, but what I was trying to say was… Listen, I *respect* you, okay? For not doing that. A lot of people would have."

Slowly, Julie let her hand fall. Tom's fingers stayed where they were, circling her wrist in a loose bracelet of warmth. Disturbed at the electricity in his touch and still unwilling to surrender her anger, she whirled away from him and found the door lock with her key.

"Hell!" he said again. "Let's stop this, Julie, once and for all."

He stood behind her. His hands moved to bracket her waist, then came around to meet over the flat warmth of her lower stomach, enclosing her fully. She could feel him against her back, feel his strength and weight, hear the vibration in his chest as he spoke.

Bending so that his jaw brushed her ear, he said in a low growl, "Our baby's growing in here. We've hardly had a minute to think about what that means. We've both had anger to let fly today. We've really hit out a few times, both of us, and for good reason.

"And we've had to think about *answers* and *solutions* as if this was some disaster. Like cancer. Or bankruptcy. But it's *not* that. It's incredible, what's happened. Our baby, Julie. Yours and mine. Growing and becoming a person right here inside you. That gives us a bond that nothing can break. A bond that's going to last forever, no matter what else happens to either of us. And we need to honor that baby bond...don't we?"

"Yes," she whispered, melting at his touch, awed by his words. "Yes, Tom, we do."

"It's what makes the world turn. It's why the human race goes on getting up in the mornings."

"I know. I know." She was close to tears, her whole being alive with the primal connection he'd spoken of.

And then, very gently, before she quite knew what was happening, he turned her into his arms and bent his face to find her mouth.

At first, the pressure of his lips was gentle, almost questioning. It sent fire through her, and her response was instant, instinctive and hungry. With her body's sensitivity heightened by pregnancy she felt every fold and seam of his clothing pressed against her length and every degree of the male heat beneath.

The wooden porch under their feet creaked as he bent lower to taste her more deeply, and his arms wound tighter, holding her so close that she could have lost consciousness and still not fallen.

As if she'd have fainted! Her nerve endings had never felt more alive, more aware. Here were his hips, hard and strong and male, pressing against her waist. Here were his thighs, rock-firm against her own, brushing her skirt across her legs as their kiss made both of them sway and rock in rhythm. And here, above all, was his sweet-tasting mouth, demanding, promising, taking and giving all at the same time.

"Julie, damn it, Julie, is it *possible* we didn't know each other before today?" he asked her huskily. "It *isn't!* It's like this is amnesia. We *must* have made love to make a baby, only something happened to make us forget until just now. That's how it feels to me. I can almost see you, lying naked in my bed with me filling you. I can hear you and smell you and taste you. I can *feel* what it must have been like to make love to you. Is that crazy?"

"No," she said against his lips. "It's not crazy. It's how I feel, too. It's the baby, Tom."

''The baby. You *have* to marry me, then, if that's what sharing a baby can do,'' he said.

He captured her mouth again, and didn't ask for an answer, but she gave him one with her kiss.

They would marry. He was right. At the moment, it was the only thing in the world that made any sense.

Chapter Four

Tom was standing there.

After spending one racking afternoon and evening with Tom Callahan, Julie hadn't seen him for
three days, and she was quite prepared to discover
that every one of last Friday's vivid impressions of
the man was wrong. But now, standing at the arrival
gate at the Albany airport, she knew they hadn't
been.

There were just a handful of people meeting the
sparsely filled flight, and he was nearly a head taller
than all of them. He was like a magnet pulling her
gaze. When he caught sight of her, his face broke
into a smile of recognition, but it quickly faded, and
she could see that his strong jaw was held tightly.
She knew her own face was still and tense, also.
Out of everything that had already happened be-

tween them, this now suddenly felt like the most unreal moment of all.

He didn't move forward, just stood there, steady as a rock, waiting. Walking toward him, she couldn't take her eyes off his face and didn't notice the flowers he held until he lifted them up and held them out to give to her.

Roses. A dozen of them, apricot pink shaking out to warm cream as the petals unfurled.

"I know by tradition they should be red," he said. It was almost an apology, and she realized that this was every bit as hard for him as it was for her. "But this creamy, peachy tone at their hearts reminded me so much of your skin, and so…"

"They're beautiful. Just beautiful. Thank you."

She took them at once and buried her face in them to drink their faint, cool scent, and only when she raised her head again and looked at him did she begin to wonder. Had he made such an apparently thoughtful gesture purely because it gave both of them a reason not to touch? Provided a fragile, prickly barrier?

If so, then she should probably thank him for that, as well. With her memory of the kiss they had shared late on Friday night still incredibly vivid, the very idea of touching him was dangerous.

Cradling the lush flowers as she started down the concourse, Julie was deeply conscious of Tom at her side. She could sense the athletic ease with which his body moved, could hear the soft friction of his denim jeans as thigh brushed thigh with each stride. And she couldn't think of a thing to say as a distraction.

"Tired?" he queried, the word caring despite its brevity.

"No," she assured him. "I'm feeling pretty good. Marcia hardly let me do anything." She and Marcia Snow had spent the past three days winding up all the final, poignant details of Loretta's life. Her clothes. Her unpaid bills. Her large assortment of impulsively purchased possessions.

As well, Julie had spent most of yesterday at her own apartment, a four-month sublet she'd taken when she arrived in Philly at the end of March. She'd planned to find something more permanent, but that wouldn't be necessary now. She would be living with Tom, dividing her time, as he did during the summer months, between Philadelphia and upstate New York.

"Good," he drawled. "She was following orders. Did it help with the nausea? Did you manage to eat properly? Did you take your vitamins?"

Suddenly, his concern grated on her. All those questions, fired off one after the other!

Perhaps if they *had* touched when they'd greeted each other a few minutes earlier, she might not have snapped at him. But she was feeling isolated, separated from him by the burden of the flowers she was carrying, and the baby she was carrying, too.

"Don't panic, Tom." Her tone was biting. "I'm doing the best I can to incubate your child in optimal conditions. And as for the *flowers*—"

"Hey!" He stopped abruptly, forcing her to stop as well.

He touched her shoulder and pulled her around to face him. His dark eyes contained an angry glint.

"That's *not* what I meant!" he said urgently. "I was concerned for *you!* I don't want you feeling the way you felt on Friday for the next two months or more. I want you to look after yourself, for your own sake as much as for the baby's. And what is it about the flowers, for heck's sake?"

"Didn't you give them to me just to make a barrier?" she accused. "So we couldn't—wouldn't have to touch?"

"That's ridiculous, Julie!"

"I'm sorry," she insisted. "It felt that way."

"I'll *show* you how ridiculous it is!"

Since she hadn't even begun to guess what he intended, the light swat of his hand against the dark green tissue wrap knocked the roses easily from her hands and sent them careening across the polished floor of the concourse to lie unheeded against the bland wall. A second later, he'd pulled her into his arms and lowered his mouth to within one lethal half-inch of hers.

"You think we should have kissed, do you?" She felt his warm, fresh breath brushing her lips. "That I should have held the flowers aside, and…let's see. Swept you off your feet and covered your mouth with mine? Something like that?"

"No. Tom, I—"

"No, you're right. You're absolutely, completely

right. Of course we should have kissed.'' His mouth was so close to hers now she could hardly have stuck a rose petal in between. ''I'll remedy the inexcusable oversight right now,'' he muttered, his voice husky and his tone ominous. His lips parted and closed over hers.

Julie had thought, over the past few days, that her memory of his kiss was almost as vivid as the real thing. It had kept her awake at night, ambushed her out of the blue during the day and made her insides coil each time.

Experiencing the real thing again, she immediately knew she'd been wrong. Memory was nothing like reality. This was...

Was it only because he was making such a deliberate performance of it? His arms were wrapped around her, and one hand was splayed with flagrant possession over the taut curves of her behind, cupping and caressing, stroking the sensitive crease at the top of her thigh. His mouth went from tasting her to devouring her, and the low growls of satisfaction that vibrated deep in his throat suggested that he'd hungered for this moment and nothing else for days.

''Tom, no!'' she mumbled against his lips.

Squirming, she tried to free her hips from their locked position against his thighs, but that only made her even more aware of the hard, lean length of him. She tried to arch her head back, shut her lips tight and escape the melting heaven of his kiss, but he chased after her with his gorgeous mouth and threaded his fingers into her hair to anchor her in place, making her tingle all over with the gesture.

She gave a ragged sigh and surrendered to the warm rain of feeling drumming inside her. But she couldn't let it last. What was he trying to prove?

Asserting her will once more, she finally succeeded in breaking apart their joined mouths, but he only took shameless advantage of her movement to trail a line of fire with his lips all the way down her throat. She gasped, and this time his name came out as a breathy moan. "Oh, Tom…"

"That's enough of that, I guess," he said huskily, vaguely, as if he'd almost lost the plot, as well.

Then he seemed to snap into control. She wished she could do the same. With one swift movement, he released her.

"I was going to save this," he went on. "But since you obviously feel that the flowers weren't enough, that my greeting was inadequate and inappropriate…" The wicked glint in his eyes froze her. What on earth was coming next? "Perhaps I'd better give it to you now."

He thrust a hand deep into his jeans pocket, pulled out a small black velvet box and flipped it open. Again, Julie gasped.

It was a ring. Almost dazzling against its black satin bed, the champagne solitaire diamond seemed to glow with its own light, and the white gold setting was as smooth and shimmering as flame.

"It's—I—I can't take this," she said. It was

barely a whisper. "How can I accept something as beautiful as this?"

But he ignored her completely, unhooking the treasure from its box and taking her hand in a caressing grip, then slipping the ring onto her finger. It fit with smug precision, grazing her knuckle lightly on the way past so that she knew it wouldn't be quite as easy to get off again. Almost as if the ring knew it belonged.

No, that was ridiculous!

Mesmerized, she gazed at it, her hand resting on Tom's, and he said with—she could almost have sworn—a catch in his throat, "I'm not very original. It's almost the same color as the roses. But somehow it's a color that seems so right for you, Julie." His forefinger stroked her hand with feather-light caresses, like a sable-tipped paintbrush on her skin.

"Tom, I can't take—"

"*Don't* say it! My parents will expect a ring, okay? Do you *want* everyone to mistrust our engagement?"

"No, of course I don't!"

He'd only done it to keep his parents happy. She should have known. She pulled her hand away, feeling a senseless, burning disappointment. How had she let herself get so caught up in the moment when clearly it was a charade? "Of course I don't," she repeated in a wooden tone.

"Then live with it!" His eyes blazed.

He was right, of course. She knew it. Right about

the whole thing. There was no point in doing this if they didn't do it properly. So why was she feeling so bruised?

Angry, too.

She was still searching for a biting retort when she heard a voice beside her. "Excuse me, honey, but I just had to pick these up before someone takes 'em or tramples 'em." A gray-haired elderly woman was tapping Julie insistently on the arm. "They're yours, aren't they?"

"I, uh, yes." She turned, flustered, took the roses and cradled them in the crook of her right arm. "Thank you very much."

"They're beautiful. That ring must really be something to have made you drop 'em like that." It was an eager hint.

Helplessly, Julie held out her left hand and heard the woman's crows of admiration. Tom's arm was around her shoulder, just like a proud, eagerly possessive fiancé.

There was a small silence, in which Julie became aware that the elderly woman wasn't the only person to have witnessed the scene. She saw two covert smiles, one set of carefully lowered eyelashes and a pair of hands, a foot or two below a big grin, that looked as if they just might be about to break out clapping.

Tom had noticed, too. "Sorry, but you might as well get used to it," he said to her in a muttered aside, dropping his arm from her shoulder. Then he said, "Let's go check the baggage carousel, shall we?"

Julie could only nod weakly. She didn't protest any more. She'd calmed down. That swollen, melting feeling on her lips was beginning to fade. He was right about the ring. People would expect it.

Tom had his hand in the small of her back as he guided her to the baggage claim carousel. She would have said the sensation was overpowering if she hadn't experienced the real meaning of that word when he'd kissed her. It was lucky she didn't want to protest any more, because she wasn't sure that the words would have come.

Tom reached the carousel a few paces ahead of her. He'd grabbed an errant baggage cart on the way, and he lifted suitcases onto it as Julie pointed them out to him.

She couldn't help noticing the effortless bulge of his biceps and saw that Tom again drew glances from strangers, both female and male. She wasn't surprised. He wore blue jeans, a white T-shirt and brown, elastic-sided boots, but there was something about him—a presence, a sense of ease and confidence and hard-earned success—that would arouse interest and curiosity wherever he went.

The efficient, unhurried way he loaded her suitcases suggested he'd done the same thing dozens of times before, in a dozen different airports around the globe.

I guess I'll get used to it, she thought, then realized Tom had said the same thing a few minutes ago.

"That's it?" he asked.

She nodded, then said as they headed for the exit, "What did you mean just now when you said I should get used to it?"

"The attention," he answered. "When people think there's romance in the air, I've noticed, they turn up for the free show. Mom's pretty good, but I have a couple of cousins…"

"Cousins?"

He gave a shrug of apology. "Look, I know the last thing either of us wants is a lavish event, but Mom and Dad both have family that they're close to. I know what's going to happen when they hear about the wedding. It being so close and all, they're going to want to pitch in and get involved."

"Involved." She could only echo him blankly.

"I've been making some calls," he confessed. "This is wedding season, Julie. All the halfway decent function centers and catering firms are booked solid, and most of the pretty ordinary ones, too. We've basically got two choices, as I see it. We can sneak off and get married on our own—which I know would hurt my parents and make them ask a lot of questions—or we can make it a family party in my parents' backyard with a bring-your-own casserole dinner."

She laughed. "Are you serious? But you're—" She bit back the blunt word, realizing how it would sound.

"I'm what?" he asked.

"Rich," she finished abruptly, and, yes, it sounded bad. Even worse than she'd thought.

"Oh, so we should spend accordingly? You fancy that life-style, do you?" His tone was mild, but she sensed his anger and flaring distrust.

"No," she answered truthfully. "Actually, I don't. Not particularly. I'd be daunted by a big society wedding. But I thought your family—"

"My father's a doctor—a family practice specialist in a neighborhood that doesn't have a lot of cash to spend on fancy health insurance. My mother used to be a nurse, but she hasn't worked since my older brother was born. That's over thirty years ago. Neither of them comes from a moneyed background.

"Yes, we've got money now through the software company I started with Patrick. The whole family has shares these days, and my brother Connor works with us full-time, as well. But you'll notice I'm not wearing Armani shoelaces and blowing my nose on gold monogrammed tissues. If you have a problem with that—"

"Tom, I don't," she insisted quietly. "I'm sorry. I was making assumptions, and I shouldn't have. I love the idea of people bringing a casserole to contribute to our wedding feast, and if I'm scared—I *am* scared!—it's only about the idea of all those people looking at us and smiling at us and curious about us, like that woman was just now, and maybe wondering what's really going on. And maybe *guessing,* so that what's...started to grow... between us, because of the baby, gets shattered before it even begins.'' She looked at him, letting the appeal show in her face. "That's all.''

Tanned, relaxed and happy—by Friday evening that was exactly how Tom felt. They'd had two and a half perfect days together during which there had been an unspoken agreement between them not to mention anything that might rock the boat—which, incidentally, was an apt expression, as he'd taken her sailing on Lake George for most of today.

So they hadn't mentioned the wedding, hadn't mentioned the prenuptial agreement, which his lawyers had been drawing up, hadn't even mentioned the baby much. Somehow they'd both just known how important it was to keep these two days apart from all that—from the practicalities and the potential problems. Like a honeymoon, this was an interlude that existed without reference to day-to-day life.

As far as honeymoons went, it was the closest they were going to get. Callahan Systems was gearing up for a major product launch in September. It was doubtful whether Tom would get much more time up here this summer. Not that a real honeymoon fitted their unique situation, anyway.

In fact, he was sorry the word had even entered his head, because it conjured up pictures of real honeymoons that were far too vivid and enticing.

This was another area in which they hadn't

needed to agree out loud on what was right. Since Wednesday, at the airport, they'd barely touched, let alone kissed, and, heaven help him, why on earth had he kissed her *then?*

The memory of it threatened to drown him, at times, with its sheer power.

He'd been, to put it bluntly, running scared that day, waiting for her at the arrival gate. Friday, that day of revelation and emotion and decision, had been so shocking and so unreal that he totally doubted the closeness they'd achieved as they said good-night, and Saturday morning had consisted only of brief, practical arrangements. As the first passengers had begun to appear from her flight, he'd looked for her intently, almost afraid he might not recognize her. She couldn't possibly possess the exceptional looks and bearing he remembered.

And then, suddenly, there she was, just as grace-ful, just as long-legged, just as glowing as memory had told him. He'd positively *thrown* the flowers at her. She'd been right in what she said that day. It *did* give him an easy way to avoid her touch, al-though he hadn't seen it that way at the time. It definitely hadn't been his impulse for buying them.

But then she'd angered him with her defensive-ness and suspicion, and deep down he knew this was because she'd been holding up a mirror to him. He was feeling exactly those things, bristling with mistrust and uncertainty. It wasn't comfortable. It wasn't comfortable at all!

So he'd made that blatant, extravagant performance of knocking aside the flowers, taking her in his arms, covering her mouth with his and giving her the ring. It absolutely served him right, he was able to concede, that their kiss had escaped his control in seconds and heated to boiling point and that the memory of how her body felt against his had been punishing him relentlessly ever since.

Touching her in any way over the past two days would have been quite disastrous. Instead, he'd done everything possible to distract himself—her, too, maybe—from thinking about it.

He and Julie had agreed that his parents, then hers, would be the first, apart from Marcia, to be told the news. The moment of telling was approaching fast.

Today's sailing had tired Julie, and she'd disappeared upstairs for a nap as soon as they got home. But he could hear sounds up there now. She was awake and getting ready to come down. Tom's heart lurched sickly against his rib cage. Mom had said they'd be leaving to drive up here straight after lunch and hoped to arrive by seven. It was almost that now.

Don had left the second boat, a good-size but rather elderly Sportsman, tied up for them on the mainland. Was that the sound of its outboard motor slowing to idling speed? Tom rose and began to pace the room restlessly, his ears straining to attach meaning to what he could hear. From upstairs came the sound of water running. And were those voices on the dock?

Could he and Julie possibly carry this off convincingly, or would it all end in anxious questions and unwanted advice?

He'd told Mom and Dad about Loretta's death by phone last Thursday, right after Julie had called with the news, and he'd been easily able to mentally fill in all the unsaid things at the other end of the line. His parents had never trusted Loretta, or liked her. He *didn't* want them to know she was in any way involved in this. That fact need not come out for months.

Sounds were more discernible now. Upstairs, the door to Julie's private bathroom had opened, and he could hear her moving in her room. That was definitely the Sportsman's motor, and when it cut out he could hear his dad's voice. "Liam, grab that bag, will you?"

"Hurry up, Julie," Tom muttered.

He didn't have time to work out why it was important, but somehow he wanted Julie to reach him first so they could have one more moment alone together, just one moment more, before the dirt hit the fan. He wanted it so much, in fact, that he started up the stairs two at a time to go in search of her. Just to squeeze her hands, meet her eyes, ask her one final time, "Are you sure you really want this?"

Too late. The front door opened, and he heard his mother's voice. "Tom, we're here!"

Reluctantly, he turned and went to greet them.

Julie saw them gathered and heard them talking

as she came down the stairs. Her gaze locked and held at once with Tom's. He was taller than his father, taller than the teenager who must be his youngest brother Liam, and it was easy for him to look at her over their heads.

"Here comes Julie," she heard him say, his deep voice husky with strain, and his mother's dark head whirled. To Julie's ears, her footsteps sounded ridiculously loud. No wonder they were all looking.

"Julie?" Mrs. Callahan said. With a caring mother's instinct, she'd picked up on the electricity in the air at once. "Who's—?"

"Hello, Mrs. Callahan, Dr. Callahan." Julie arrived at the little group as she spoke. "Hello, Liam," she added.

She and Tom reached out to each other automatically. They hadn't planned this moment, but what happened next fitted perfectly. His arm slipped around her waist, and her hand came to rest on his shoulder so that their sides were pressed together. It felt like a lifeline, vital and supporting and warm, and when Tom spoke, what he had to say seemed surprisingly right and easy.

"Mom, Dad, Liam, this is Julie, the woman I'm going to marry."

Beth Callahan gasped. "*Marry?* Thomas Edward Callahan! Could you at least let me sit down and offer me a glass of water before you spring a piece of news like that on me?"

He smiled crookedly. "Well, you're right, I didn't intend to tell you that way, but since I could see from your face that you were already pole-vaulting to conclusions on the subject, it seemed best to put you out of your misery right away.''

"Julie." Mrs. Callahan turned to her with a help-less expression and a smile as wry as her son's. "You've caught me at a terrible disadvantage, but may I kiss you anyway?" She did so, a quick, warm squeeze and peck, then turned to Tom. "I just don't know what to say."

"Say nothing, darling," Dr. Callahan suggested dryly. "Just absorb it in stunned silence like I'm doing."

Both Tom's parents looked like they had in the photo Julie remembered him showing her a week ago. She could still see it vividly in her mind. Beth Callahan was older, but even warmer in person, and Jim had a perpetual helpless sort of twinkle in his eyes as if he wasn't quite sure how he'd gotten to be the father of eight grown sons and didn't at all know how to proceed.

"I don't know what the fuss is about," Liam complained. "They're getting married. That's usu-ally supposed to be good news, isn't it? Nice to meet you, Julie, and congratulations, both of you."

He stuck out his hand, and Julie shook it.

"'Bout time we had a natural blond on the team.''

"Liam!" said his mother.

"I've noticed that the size of a woman's en-gagement ring is always directly proportional to the size of the wedding they want. Show us your left hand, Julie,'' Liam continued, clearly on a roll.

Laughing, she did so. She knew Tom's narrowed gaze was fixed on her. He was wondering how she was handling Liam. She was handling him just fine! His brash teenage joshing was going a long way toward making this easier for everyone. A little goofy-looking, and with skin that wasn't as blemish-free as he'd doubtless have liked, he'd mature into another good-looking Callahan man by his mid-twenties, Julie guessed.

He whistled at the sight of the gorgeous champagne diamond in its white gold setting and calculated aloud. ''On the strength of that, I'd say two hundred guests, eleven bridesmaids, engraved swizzle sticks and lobster for the entree.''

''Wrong,'' Tom retorted. ''That's the other thing. Well, one of the other things we've got to tell you. We, uh, didn't want to wait around and we didn't want a huge event. The wedding's a week from tomorrow.''

Beth Callahan moaned. ''Do I get any sort of a say in this?''

''I'm almost thirty-four years old, Mother dear.''

''Yes…''

''And I checked with Dad's receptionist about your schedule for the next few weeks.''

Jim Callahan was consulting a small pocket diary. ''Morning or afternoon?'' he asked, giving a quizzical glance over the top of his bifocals.

''Afternoon, I expect,'' Tom replied. ''We were

waiting till we'd talked it over with you before we finalized the details.''

His mother raised her eyes to the ceiling. "Thank heaven for small mercies!"

"Afternoon?" Dr Callahan said thoughtfully, still studying his diary. "Well, my receptionist was right. I'm free after eleven. That's handy. Shall I pencil you in for the whole rest of the day?"

"Probably wise," Tom agreed.

"Now, Beth," his father continued calmly. "Perhaps we should eat. By the looks of you, you're not fit to do any more talking about weddings on an empty stomach. Has that housekeeper of yours fixed something wonderful, Tom?"

"No, I've, uh, given her the last couple of days off," Tom explained.

Although he hadn't said so to Julie directly, she knew he'd done this in order for them to be alone together as much as possible. That sort of forethought and sensitivity was something she was starting to appreciate and count on.

"So I just stuck a couple of frozen pizzas in the oven," Tom said. "Will that do?"

"As if I'll even *notice!*" Beth Callahan said. "Tom, you see these gray hairs?" She threaded a strand through her fingers. "I swear they weren't there five minutes ago. Julie, you ought to know something about this man, if you haven't found it out already. He has the most horrible habit of *springing* things on you. Do you know the way he and Patrick let us know their company was finally in the black after nine years of barely breaking even?''

''No, I don't.'' She laughed, feeling a secret and almost guilty surge of delight at the prospect of hearing all his mother's very worst stories about the man she'd agreed to marry.

''They just handed us a check for the outstanding balance on our mortgage. It was over sixty thousand dollars, while I'd still been losing sleep over whether they could pay the electricity bill for their office space that month!''

''And you were right to worry,'' Tom retorted cheerfully. ''A week before that, before that first contract with Metroplus was signed, we couldn't pay our bills. Now, let's eat, shall we? Mom, do you mind dishing up?''

''But I haven't unpacked, I haven't—''

''Later, later.'' He waved the three Callahans through to the kitchen but held Julie back.

''Don't get carried away, you two,'' Liam admonished.

''There's a fire extinguisher on the kitchen wall if you think we might need it,'' Julie retorted at once, then melted at Tom's appreciative shout of laughter.

Liam was laughing, too, as he disappeared into the kitchen.

Tom waited, holding her lightly in his arms. Fulfilling expectations, Julie knew. She wished it didn't feel so wonderful and so right when they both knew it was only a sham.

"I think that went okay, don't you?" he said softly as soon as the coast was clear.

"It went great," she agreed, wondering why there was suddenly a lump in her throat.

"Liam's got a mouth on him these days, hasn't he, though? He loves it when people sass him back, so keep it up."

"That's not an act, Tom. I like him. And your mom and dad."

She smiled at him, and he bent to brush a quick kiss across her mouth. Startled, she instinctively parted her lips, and instead of ending the moment, Tom was tricked into tasting her, clinging to her mouth for a moment longer before they both pulled away.

Julie's heart was pounding. It wasn't fair that a little kiss like that could do this to her!

Unable to meet his look, she glanced up and saw his mother pause just outside the swing door to the kitchen. She obviously didn't want to interrupt.

"Just wondering about a salad, Tom," Beth said apologetically, and she couldn't quite keep an indulgent smile off her face. Julie was blushing ferociously. Wasn't this all unfolding exactly as it might have done if they were wildly in love?

"Sure," Tom answered, and went to the kitchen.

They ate ten minutes later, grouped casually around the solid wood table, and the talk was mainly of family news and Tom's ideas for the informal wedding he and Julie had agreed on. As yet, the baby had not been mentioned. Tom wanted to share that news with his parents alone first. It was an announcement that didn't need the treatment of Liam's mouth, as Tom had put it.

First, though, Julie wanted to call her mom.

"Use my office," Tom told her. Beth Callahan was clearing away the dishes while her husband made coffee.

"Thanks."

Julie appreciated the chance for privacy. This was going to be a difficult call. She'd felt so shut out of her mother's life since her mom's marriage to Matt Kady a year and a half ago, and if this wedding was founded on love she'd have looked on it as the perfect opportunity for the two of them to get close again.

Mom had spent years weaving captivating fantasies about Julie's wedding day, entrancing her in her early teens.

"You'll have the whole church filled with the scent of orange blossom, sweetheart, and your dress will be so huge there'll be no room in the limo for anyone else. Of course you'll be marrying some fabulous man, the prince of your dreams, and I'll be there in a lilac dress with a lilac corsage. Your bouquet will be white lilies and roses. And you won't mind if I cry, darling, because they'll be tears of happiness. My daughter, my own little girl, *getting married…*"

The reality would be so different.

But perhaps that wasn't important. Perhaps this wedding would still offer the chance for closeness.

Just before the ceremony, while Mom helped Julie dress, she'd tell her about the baby.

Breathless and close to tears, Julie punched in her mother's number, heard the familiar voice and stumbled through her announcement and her explanation of their plans.

"Next Saturday? Oh, sweetheart..."

"You can't come," Julie guessed, disappointment making her stomach plunge. She forced it aside. With such short notice, it wasn't fair to resent it.

"Sweetheart, you don't understand. Matt needs *me*. He has an audition. She overflowed with details then finished. There's no way I can make it. Just no way. I'm truly sorry." Her voice rose to a high-pitched, syrupy coo. "I truly am!"

Is this just me? Julie wondered when she'd put down the phone. Am I selfish to think maybe my wedding is more important than preparing Matt for an audition? Can he really be that dependent on her?

She fought hard to hide what she felt. If Tom guessed how much this hurt, if she had to deal with Beth Callahan's tactful attempts to hide her astonishment at Mom's priorities...

She wanted to protect her mother, too. Maybe her mom was right. Maybe Julie didn't understand. She'd certainly been told so often enough since her mother's remarriage.

"They can't make it, unfortunately," she said in a neutral tone. "They're working on a movie."

Liam was young enough to be impressed. "A movie? Wow!"

Beth said mildly, "I don't suppose there's flexibility in the scheduling with something like that, is there?"

"I'm afraid not," Julie agreed.

Tom moved restlessly, and she caught his look. She seemed to have become attuned to the language of his body over the past few days—perhaps because she was constantly aware of it. She knew he was uncomfortable. And she knew why. Any minute now, Beth would ask if the wedding couldn't be timed so Julie's side of the family could make it, and neither of them wanted the revelation about the baby to come out of a messy discussion on scheduling.

To head off the possibility, Tom said quickly to Liam, "Come into my office and look at that game." It was the newest product being developed by the Callahan Systems computer games division.

"Write down your comments, Liam," Tom added. "I've told Patrick I don't think the background to the graphics is detailed enough, but he disagrees." He shut the office door. "That should keep him busy for a while, I hope."

As soon as coffee was poured, Beth looked expectantly at Jim, as if they'd somehow silently agreed he'd be the one to voice the issue, and he said quietly at once, "So, you two, what is it that you're not telling us?"

Tom didn't try to dress the issue up in fancy

finery. He sat beside Julie, and as usual she felt cherished by the way he touched her, taking her hand and laying it on his thigh, then covering it warmly with his. She *shouldn't* feel that way! It was dangerous. He was only doing it for his parents' benefit.

"We're having a baby," he said, "And we're thrilled about it."

"But if it wasn't for the baby—" again, it was Jim "—you wouldn't be getting married so soon?"

"No."

"Or you wouldn't be getting married at all?"

Julie felt Tom flinch. His tension zapped straight into her like an electric current. He stood restlessly and went to lean against the hardwood mantel above the broad stone fireplace, his face tight and serious.

"I can't answer that, Dad," he said honestly. "We're faced with this situation and we're doing what feels right, that's all. We're very happy, aren't we, Julie? And very excited about the baby."

"Yes," she answered, laying a hand over her stomach. "More than I'd thought possible."

They talked for some time longer. There were lots of questions from Beth Callahan about Julie and her family, but knowing what motivated them, she didn't resent them, and when Beth was given a none-too-subtle hint from her husband about saving everyone some time and hiring a private detective, Beth laughed and apologized.

"Julie, you should have told me fifteen minutes ago to mind my own business!"

"It *is* your business," Julie answered seriously. "And I'm very glad it is."

She was thinking of Mom again, and realized she didn't even ask about Tom, couldn't even spare the time from her own life to ask about the man she's marrying.

"And *I'm* glad," Beth was saying, "that you think so. Your baby deserves this—deserves to come into the world as part of a family, and to have that security. Oh...dear...I didn't mean to make you cry."

"You didn't," said Julie, grabbing a tissue and blotting her eyes frantically. "I'm sorry. It's silly. I just agree with you, that's all, and it's so good to hear someone else say it."

"But hasn't Tom...?"

"Yes, him, too. Tom believes in family, too. That's why I—" She stopped, horrified. She'd almost said, "That's why I love him." But that couldn't be true. It *couldn't*.

Beth didn't seem to need a completed sentence. "I know," she said, squeezing Julie's hand. "Family's important. Has Tom told you about our son Adam?"

"Just a little."

"He's an idealist. He got involved with this girl Cherie because he thought he could do something for her, and it was too late by the time he found out he couldn't. He wanted to marry her, but she refused. She skipped town twice during the pregnancy, but both times she came back and Adam was at Amy's birth, at least, thank goodness. She was such a tiny, fragile thing. Almost three months premature.

"Then Cherie abandoned Amy in the hospital and Adam was all set to raise her himself, only just before she was due to be discharged Cherie came back again, took the baby and disappeared. Can you imagine what that's doing to him?"

"It must be unbearable."

"And what it's doing to us?"

"I know."

"The thing is, the way Cherie is, we can't even be sure the baby's physically safe. I see her, sometimes, in my imagination, left locked alone in a car..."

"Oh, no!"

"Or not getting fed properly, or getting abandoned somewhere and not being found in time—"

She broke off, unable to go on, then said some moments later, "So bless you for giving us some *good* news! And please work hard at what you've got..."

"I will. We..." She looked at Tom. He was talking to his father now, over by the fireplace and hadn't heard any of this. "We will," she finished firmly, while knowing she had no right to make such a promise for him.

Chapter Five

"Well, when the going gets tough, the tough get married," was how Liam had phrased it a week ago when Tom and Julie had told him privately about the baby.

The flippant new take on an old cliché had been going around Julie's head ever since. Maybe it was true. She hoped so. She needed to believe in her own toughness today. Her wedding day, and not one of her friends or relatives in attendance.

Pacing the bedroom in the sprawling old Callahan house where she'd spent the past few nights and where she was supposed to be getting dressed for the ceremony, Julie stared reality in the face. To the eyes of the large Callahan clan, this must look like just what it was. Odd. Wrong. Sending out large, loud signals that this wasn't your average wedding.

Desperately wanting a friend, any friend, Julie had called her college roommate, Erin, in California earlier in the week, only to find that Erin was on a summer grad student program in Spain. She'd called her best friend since high school, Laurie, and Laurie would have come if she hadn't been booked as maid of honor at her older sister's wedding the same day.

But she wasn't going to blow it out of proportion. There was nothing shameful in being alone. It was just...lonely.

Which didn't explain why she'd hidden her feelings from Tom so carefully all week. He'd asked her more than once if everything was all right, and she'd made some bright, offhand reply each time. He'd asked if she was upset about her mother not coming and had offered to delay the ceremony, which they knew was impossible, given everyone's commitments.

And she'd gently refused Beth Callahan's offer of help in getting dressed, knowing that Beth had enough to do as hostess without having to shut herself in here and fuss over a dress and a bride with stage fright.

"I've gotten dressed on my own every day of my life since I was four years old, so there's no reason I can't do it now!"

A knock sounded at the door hard on the heels of her last words, spoken defiantly to the mirror. A pretty young woman of about eighteen stood there.

"I'm Jeri," she said. "One of the cousins. Tom

sent me to see if you needed help getting dressed, but if you've already got someone with you…'' She frowned uncertainly and wiped a strand of brown hair from her face. She had deep green eyes, which looked far too sparkly for the safety of the male sex.

''There's no one,'' Julie explained. ''You caught me talking to myself!'' She laughed. It didn't bother her to admit to this mild craziness. Just hearing those words, ''Tom sent me,'' had done wonders to lift her mood.

So why was she suddenly crying uncontrollably?

Jeri knew.

''You're pregnant, aren't you?'' she said sympathetically, darting into the room and closing the door behind her.

Julie nodded. Her shoulders were shaking, and gulping back the sobs only threatened to give her hiccups. Accepting defeat, she let them come.

''Don't worry. I came prepared,'' Jeri said.

Julie noticed the big box of tissues in her hand. Jeri grabbed a large handful of them and held them out.

''Thanks.''

''Tom's idea. Don't thank me. I tell you, he's a doll, but of course you'd know that better than anyone.''

''I—I guess I would.'' She stopped crying.

''Okay?'' Jeri asked.

''Sometimes I feel like I've turned into the weather channel,'' she admitted.

"I can imagine. I mean, *ordinary* brides cry, right? I guess pregnant ones weep buckets."

"So does everyone—"

"Know you're pregnant?" Jeri finished cheerfully. "Probably! Liam told Danny, and Danny told Jody, and Jody told me. But then I also heard it from my cousin Helen, who says Connor told her, so—"

"I get the picture." Julie had recognized the names of several of Tom's brothers.

"Sorry. Do you mind? *We* don't. It's kind of romantic, isn't it?"

"Everyone knowing?"

"Being pregnant and getting married. And as for everyone knowing…"

"Better than having everyone whispering behind their hands, I guess," Julie said.

"The Callahans aren't like that," Jeri said firmly. "So shall I stay? Tom said I *had* to, on pain of death."

The weather channel flipped to a different climate again. Warm. Sunny. With little white fluffy clouds of hope and happiness. "Well, if he said that…"

"Aha! An obedient wife! Are you planning to say that in the vows? Love, honor and obey?"

"Not exactly." They'd gone over their vows, making some changes on the traditional phrases so they could speak the words without hypocrisy. That was only three days ago, but already it seemed weeks distant with all the frantic whirl of everything they'd had to do.

"Tom's here, then?" It suddenly struck her. "Is it later than I think?"

"Well, in six minutes and—" Jeri studied her watch "—thirty-five seconds, you'll be late. But for a bride, that's practically compulsory."

"Six minutes?"

"And twenty-eight seconds," Jeri told her helpfully. Then she added, "Better start by washing your face. Your eyes look red."

Between the two of them, they had Julie ready in sixteen minutes. And twenty-five seconds. Julie hadn't wanted much makeup and refused any fragrance. The scent of cosmetics was one of many things that brought on her increasing nausea these days. Jeri was disappointed, but when Julie remembered what Tom had said about her skin, she knew he wouldn't mind.

And so she came downstairs to the waiting crowd of Callahan family and friends gathered in the back garden, her cream silk dress swinging around her ankles and a garland of peach-hued roses in her upswept hair.

At first her smile felt like it had been stitched in place, wide and stiff and unnatural, but when she saw Tom, in his dark suit, turn and catch sight of her, it faded altogether. Slowly passing between the parted ranks of wedding guests, with eyes for Tom alone, she could only show what she felt—a brief rush of fear, then trust settling inside her like a warm blanket, and finally a calm sense of hope.

Tom felt his heart swell almost painfully as he watched her approach. The ten long minutes he'd waited for her since taking up his position beneath the arched white wooden trellis of climbing roses had dragged like hours.

Since Julie had no official bridesmaid, he had no official best man. He'd asked Adam to safeguard the two plain gold wedding bands they'd chosen. As those awful minutes ticked by, he'd been very aware of Adam standing just a few feet away. Adam, who'd waited endless weeks for his baby daughter to be fit enough to leave the hospital, only to learn, when he visited her the day before she was due for discharge, that her unstable mother had taken her and vanished without trace.

The torment showed like a shadow in Adam's handsome face, aging him noticeably, and it made ten minutes of waiting seem laughably easy by comparison. And yet…what if Julie had changed her mind, jilted Tom in the garden of his parents' home, so that *he* was about to lose a baby, too?

There had been something bothering her this past week that she wasn't admitting to, even though he'd given her several openings. Why? What was on her mind? What was she hiding? Was she getting cold feet about the wedding? About the baby? There was normally something so open about her face. That openness was emphasized by the frank, almost boyish smile that he'd seen—and deliberately tried to provoke—countless times. She wasn't the type to hide things, to layer and censor her emotions. He loved that. If the week hadn't been so impossibly hectic, he'd have found a way to get the truth from her.

But the time for that was past, and it was their wedding hour, and she was more than ten minutes late.

Then, just as he felt his nerves were stretched to breaking, the hum of the gathered crowd stilled, and there she was, with mischievous little cousin Jeri tiptoeing after her, hiding her delighted laughter behind her hands.

The ceremony passed in a blur. Father Daniel Collins, an old friend of the family, guided them through it without any disastrous stumblings or lapses of memory. Julie had to take it on trust that she'd said everything because afterward she could scarcely remember a word.

And the ceremony was only the beginning. There was the reception, with music and dancing and dozens of fragmented conversations shouted above the growing noise.

Everyone seemed to be having a whale of a time.

Julie was, too. *Would* have been, anyway, if she hadn't felt so overwhelmed. It was wonderful to be so thoroughly welcomed into such a family—only she'd met so many people now she couldn't remember anyone's name. The food was all delicious—only nothing tasted quite right these days,

with her pregnancy. No one had the slightest dif-
ficulty in thinking of what to say to her, and everyone wanted to talk to the bride—only she kept waiting for some beaming, well-meaning new relative
to ask her some question about herself and Tom
that she didn't dare answer.

And through it all there was Tom, touching her
hand as he asked if she needed another plate of
food, quickly mouthing the name of the elderly uncle she'd already been introduced to twice and still
didn't have a handle on. Roy? Ray? Rex? Tom,
catching her eye whenever he wasn't at her side, as
if her welfare was always his only concern. Tom,
grinning and fooling with his brothers the way he
had in that first family photo he'd shown her. Tom,
who was being the perfect husband.

She couldn't help wondering how it would feel
to know she would have him beside her for the rest
of their lives.

Somehow, she was starting to know it would feel
like heaven.

But it's not what he wants, she told herself. *This
is only about the baby. And if I start to think anything else, then I'm just being a fool!*

She had to get away. Muttering something about
getting another club soda, she slipped between the
guests toward the house.

The summer evening was still warm and light,
so everyone was outside or busy in the kitchen. The
rest of the house was quiet. Julie paced through the

big living room, feeling vulnerable. At any moment, someone might come in.

Tom.

I can't face him. Not until I've got this under control. I've seen it coming. I knew it could be like this. But why is it so strong today?

"Because you've just married the man, of course!" a friend might have said, if she'd had a friend with her. Or her mother.

She hurried up the stairs. Although it had five spacious bedrooms, the large house wasn't elegant. It had sheltered too many energetic boys to escape a certain degree of shabbiness and wear, but it felt wonderfully like a home, the way her mother's place in California never had. Julie had spent the past four nights here.

The big Callahan place felt just like home.

Julie went into the room she'd been using but didn't quite dare hide behind a closed door. If Tom discovered her and realized what she was hiding from...

A part of her didn't want him to discover her at all. If she could just have some time to get this into perspective. They were marrying because of the baby. This could be a strong foundation, if she was sensible. But if she *wasn't* sensible, if she fell for him, fell *hard*, with one almighty thud...

She felt herself teetering on the brink of a big, dangerous drop. It could ruin everything. He wanted a good mother for his child, one he could respect and care for in a cool sort of way, not a trembling, clinging mess of burning passion and need.

The needy part of her *did* want him to discover her. The needy part wanted him to thunder into this room *right now,* demanding to know where she'd been, slamming the door behind him, pulling her into his arms, covering her trembling mouth with his hungry one because already, after less than ten minutes, it felt like far too long since they had touched.

She heard a sound, a tiny, mewing cry. A baby, fussing gently in the room next door. She wasn't surprised. She knew that a few of the cousins had brought infants. She had heard Beth telling one mother to set up her portable crib in the spare bedroom. If someone came up now to quiet a restless baby...

Julie knew her cheeks were on fire, and a glance in the mirror showed eyes that glittered wildly. It would be bad enough if Tom saw her like this, but if some well-meaning Callahan cousin—perhaps the irrepressible Jeri's equally forthright big sister, Jill—were to pass by to comfort her crying baby and find the bride pacing in her room with her hands trembling, nervously crushing the beautiful silk of her dress in her convulsively tightened palms...

Quickly, she moved on satin-slippered feet into the next room. There were two portable cribs. They both contained babies several months old, and both were deeply and soundly asleep. The tiny fussing sound came from the bed. On it lay a much younger child, surely just a few weeks old. She was wedged carefully between two pillows, but she'd wriggled in her sleep so that one of them was nearly covering her face.

With a surge of tenderness, Julie picked her up. It was definitely a her. The pink stretchy jumpsuit and pink flannel blanket she was swaddled in left no doubt. And perhaps pregnant women did give off a special, indefinable scent of motherness, because she settled almost at once in Julie's silk-clad arms and was soon fast asleep, yawning widely as if staying awake was just too big an effort for a tired baby girl.

"Oh, you darling little thing."

Carefully, Julie laid her down again, then looked for something better than the pillows. She didn't quite trust them. They were too fat and stiff, which meant it was far too easy for the baby to wriggle beneath them. The room didn't contain many possibilities, short of poaching some space in one of the cribs. But those babies looked quite alarmingly sturdy in comparison to this little creature. They'd probably be more dangerous to her than the pillows.

There was a pink diaper bag at the foot of the bed, with a large can of powdered formula wedged into the zippered opening, but that didn't seem ideal, either. Reluctantly, Julie left the baby as she'd found her, then tiptoed from the room, hugging the growing, hidden fact of her coming child deliciously close.

"Julie. At last I've found you!"

It was Tom.

She hadn't seen him, and she gasped as his arms came tight and hard around her. "Where've you been?" he demanded huskily in her ear. She could feel the heat of his hands through the silk of her dress.

"I—" But how on earth could she tell him? *I ran away because I couldn't face you, when every moment what I feel for you gets stronger and more impossible.* "I heard a baby crying," she said. "So I went to see if I could soothe her down."

"Whose baby?" He frowned. "I'll go and get her mom."

"I don't know whose. But she's asleep now, so I guess it's fine."

She'd spoken too soon. The little mewing, fussing sound started up again, and Tom let her go. She shivered, which didn't make sense, as the house wasn't remotely cold.

"Come and show me," he said, pulling her hand. "You said her, didn't you?"

"Yes. I mean, she's as pink as a piece of cotton candy, and about that small, too."

"But Linda has Kayla outside." He calculated. "And Brad has a boy, and so does Michael." He tossed his cousins' names off confidently.

"Tom, I'm trying, but your family is *huge,*" she apologized. "I'll get it straight eventually."

"No, no that's not the problem," he said absently. "I'm just wondering—" He looked at her suddenly. "Hey! Is this why you're hiding? You don't think you're doing a bad job, do you?" he demanded.

"Of remembering everyone's names and who they are? Yes!"

"I mean, at this whole thing. At the ceremony. At being a bride."

"I—"

"Because you've been perfect, Julie." He took a step toward her, his legs at once swamped by the folds of her dress. "Everyone loves you. Everyone thinks you're beautiful," he insisted, his voice vibrating deep in his chest. "Everyone's sorry your mom and stepdad couldn't make it, because they're missing out on being so proud of you. *I'm* so proud of you. My uncle Roy told me ten minutes ago that I was the luckiest man alive, and you know what?" His voice was a whisper.

"What, Tom?" Her lips could hardly form the words.

"I'm starting to think he might be right."

He turned her into his arms and lowered his head, his mouth just inches from hers. He was going to kiss her. Not the staged kiss that had come at the end of the ceremony, passing in a brief blur of clumsy lips and whistles and cheers from the crowd, nor their other very public clinch at Albany airport last week, but a real kiss, a private kiss, like the very first they had shared, intensely felt.

She was stretching her throat and parting her lips to taste him, already feeling the melting heat inside her that seemed to ignite the moment he touched her. Their noses bumped. Their mouths were half an inch apart. She closed her eyes and felt the whisper of his warm breath.

Then the baby cried again. Her cries built to a crescendo within seconds. Julie opened her eyes to find Tom staring at her, his eyes glittering and big and dark.

"The baby," she said.

"Isn't happy, is she?"

The shrieking cries suddenly sounded dangerously muffled.

"Oh, Tom, I know what's happening," she told him. She ran across the landing at the top of the stairs.

Behind her, Tom fought his frustration. This had to be one of the outer rings of hell—to be so close to a kiss, to be racked with raging desire, and to have it stopped like that. Oh, the way Julie's body moved in that stunning dress! Even the sounds the skirt made as it swished.

Whose damned baby was it, anyway, whose parents didn't even stay within hearing range so they'd know if it cried?

"You see?" Julie was crooning when he reached her. She was going to make a brilliant mother. Her cheeks were glowing. "You see, poor little thing. I knew you'd shuffle yourself under that pillow and get yourself all upset and half suffocated. See, she's tiny, Tom. Should she really be on this bed? Why isn't she in a crib or a bassinet? Who does she belong to, anyway?''

"I—don't know," he said. His voice sounded odd. He looked at the pink diaper bag and the can of formula, then saw the folded piece of paper taped to the side of the can and tore it off impatiently. It didn't take long to read.

"Oh, Lord," he muttered. "Oh, great goodness."

"Tom, what is it?" Julie stared at him.

At first he'd gone white. Now color was flooding into his face. He threw the fluttering note to her, and she read it holding the crying baby against her shoulder. "Adam, you take her. I can't deal with it anymore, Cherie."

"It's Adam's baby," Tom said. "It's Amy." He galloped down the stairs two at a time. "Adam!" he yelled. "Where's Adam?"

"If there's one good thing about having your wedding upstaged by a lost and found baby," Tom said, "it's getting away early from the reception. I was right, wasn't I? You looked like you were ready to leave."

"I was," Julie agreed.

Although coming here, to a top-floor suite in one of Philly's best hotels, wasn't exactly what she'd had in mind. Three of Tom's brothers had been so appalled at the idea of there being no honeymoon they'd given the newlyweds two nights here as a surprise. While the drama over Amy's return had continued, Julie had packed a suitcase for the un-expected treat instead of packing to go to Tom's apartment, which had been their plan.

Patrick and Adam and Connor hadn't expected the newly married pair to need much more than bed, whirlpool and room service in the way of en-tertainment. But a couple who had no sex written into their very private prenuptial agreement re-quired a lot more serious distraction than that. Pref-erably involving other people.

Perhaps they should have stayed longer at the reception, after all. There had been quite a party in progress when they left. Adam had been in a daze, almost unable to believe that Amy was real and in his arms.

Tom must have been thinking about Adam, too.

"Let's start with this," he said, pulling a bottle of champagne out of an ice bucket. "We've got even more to celebrate now Adam has Amy back."

He thumbed the cork from the bottle, and the sparkling liquid within foamed into the two tall flutes he had waiting.

"It was all so sudden," Julie said. "One minute I was waiting for one of your cousins to come in, all apologetic about leaving her, and the next it turns out to be the best news your family has had in months."

"Maybe the best," Tom agreed as he held a champagne flute out to her, "because we were all hurting for Adam and Amy. But not the only good news. I think you and me and *our* baby come pretty high up the list, don't you?''

"Oh, yes," she answered taking the glass. "Definitely!"

He kept doing this to her—being the perfect husband and father-to-be—and she didn't know how to handle it. There was one obvious response. Surrender. Let herself fall in love. That would be easy. And impossible.

She had to hold herself back. But how? Lost in thought, she almost took a sip of her drink, then he reminded her, "We have to make a toast, Julie."

"I guess we do. Any ideas?"

"To us?" He looked at her steadily, and at once she began to drown in his gaze.

"Us," she echoed. It sounded so good. Private and special and right. Warm all over, she raised the glass to her lips, but before she tasted the dry, bubbling liquid, reality crashed in. "Us?" she repeated tightly. "Tom, there *is* no us, remember?"

It hurt to say it because she was starting to want "us" so badly.

"We're alone now," she went on. "Let's not pretend. Let's be honest to each other, at least. We're here in this suite, yes, but that's not our doing. It was great of your brothers to think of it, to want it for us, but they don't know. They don't understand the situation between us. So it's lucky there's a sofa bed, because one of us is going to be sleeping on it tonight. That's what our agreement says, and that's what we're going to stick to."

"Okay, so maybe we should forget the toast altogether," Tom answered coolly. "Forget being in
the same room with each other. Forget talking at
all. Why don't you take the bedroom and I'll take
the sofa bed? There's a TV in both rooms, so we
don't even have to watch the same channel. Is that
more like what you had in mind?"

"Yes! Why not?" she said, fuming. "I hate pre-
tence. And I need a break. Is that so hard to understand?"

"I guess not," he growled. "Take one, then.
Take the bedroom, and I'll see you in the morning."

He put down the unwanted champagne glass with
a brittle slam. Julie was surprised it didn't shatter.
He covered the distance to her suitcase in two seconds, swung it up and carried it to the bedroom.
"Is there anything more you want from room service?" he asked. His impatience was obvious,
maybe even deliberate.

"I'm fine." She lifted her chin. "And if you
need the bathroom…"

"There's a half bath here. You're on your own
till morning, Julie, since that's the way you want
it."

He was standing outside the doorway, waiting for
her to go in. How had things got this bad this fast?
She faced him and instinctively laid a hand on his
arm as she spoke.

"What do *you* want, then, Tom? Tell me!" she
demanded, fighting to keep him from seeing how

much she wanted to prolong and deepen their contact. She took her hand from his arm and balled it convulsively into a fist. "How did *you* think we'd spend tonight?"

They were standing so close she could feel the heat of him, could feel his male strength, and it was drawing her in like a magnet.

"I want—" He broke off and gave a rasping sigh between his teeth. "Hell! I don't know! This, I suppose. What we're about to do. Go to our separate beds. You're right. It's in the agreement. And we've had to do all that newlywed stuff today. Yeah, okay, we need to be alone, take some time. Good night, then, Julie. Get some sleep. I'll save the champagne."

"Drink it. I wasn't going to take more than a few sips, anyhow."

"No, Julie," he answered heavily. "Sleeping alone is one thing, but drinking alone? I don't think we've quite sunk to those depths yet. Give our marriage a few more months, okay?"

"Okay," she echoed, hardly aware of what she was saying.

She closed the door between them and fought her tears. That last barb of cynicism from him had been like the cut of a whip on her flesh, a burning slice of utterly unexpected pain. So he was expecting her to drive him to drink? Since when had he been so cold on the possibility of success in their marriage?

It was just over two weeks since he'd managed to convince her it was their baby's best chance, and now, in the space of a few minutes, he'd gone from toasting their union to predicting a painful degree of ugliness in their future.

She knew her rejection of his proposed toast was partly to blame, but there had to be more. She was numb as she made her preparations for bed, but when she finally slid between the fine cream sheets she realized that what consumed her more than anything was fatigue. She was asleep within minutes.

Tom couldn't sleep at all. For a long time, he didn't even try. Despite what he'd said about drinking alone, he downed two full flutes of the excellent champagne, brooding on what he felt and why.

What on earth had prompted those last inexcusably cynical phrases of his? What *did* he want? He'd had one horrible marriage, and he'd begun it with all the starry-eyed optimism of youth. It had been a revelation to him, back then, how sour things could get between two people when one of them wasn't prepared to work or compromise.

On the other hand, he'd seen in his parents' relationship just how *good* marriage could be, and he'd seen what was important in making it that way. This kept him, at heart, a believer. He knew it could be done, and if he *hadn't* known this, then he wouldn't have been prepared to take this outrageously bold step with Julie. He'd sensed—or thought he had—that she had something of the same understanding about what was involved.

I wanted to toast us, he realized. *I didn't want a*

reminder at that moment that it wasn't real and we
might not make it. Why did she choose that moment
to break the illusion, when the illusion was...

So good. So dangerously, impossibly good.

Maybe she'd been pretending all along, seeing
what he wanted from the mother of his child and
giving it to him. Maybe that was the thing he'd
sensed. He was a rich man, after all, worth millions.
It wouldn't be the first time an attractive woman
had remade herself in the image of what a man
wanted in order to stake a claim on his fortune.
He'd received plenty of warnings from lawyers, financial advisers, his brother Patrick.

He didn't want to distrust Julie. He didn't plan
to start doing so on no evidence, but all the same,
suddenly, for the first time, now that they were actually married, he felt vulnerable.

Chapter Six

After a healthy sleep, last night didn't matter. Julie could see it for what it was—the product of intense fatigue and stress in both of them. They'd sort it out over breakfast. She'd apologize, clarify things, touch him.

Oh, yes, definitely touch him!

She was smiling at the thought as she went to the window to pull back the heavy drapes. If the day looked nice, maybe they could eat outside at a table beneath a striped umbrella and—

She never got to finish the thought.

Pure shock, like a bucket of ice followed by a bucket of hot water, all over her. It happened so suddenly, so silently and so painlessly that she might have doubted it if the feeling hadn't been so unmistakable.

Out of the blue, she was bleeding, and all she could do for several seconds was just stand there.

When Tom's knock sounded at the door, her answer was so faint and strangled he couldn't have heard.

The door opened, and behind the dizzy roar in her ears she heard him speak. "Julie, are you—?" Then his voice broke off abruptly.

She looked at him, and for about five telltale seconds could read the unmistakable horror and accusation in his face.

"You're not pregnant. You lied all along! You were never preg—" Again Tom stopped as suddenly as if a knife had slashed off the end of the word.

Her stricken face told him what a mistake he'd made, and he knew he never would have made it if he hadn't once been married to Loretta.

Of course Julie hadn't lied. Of course she was pregnant.

Or she had been.

Perhaps she wasn't anymore.

The possibility tore at his heart, and he could already see what it was doing to her.

"Oh, hell, Julie, I'm sorry," he whispered, reaching for her. "I'm sorry I even doubted it for a second."

"That doesn't matter," she answered, shaking her head, eyes closed.

She looked so alone, his heart twisted with regret. "Not now. Just get me to a doctor," she begged.

After phoning the obstetrician his father and Adam had recommended, Tom carried Julie to the elevator. They went to the undeground parking level, where he'd put his BMW last night. It was a Sunday morning and not many people were about.

As if *that* mattered, either!

Julie hadn't spoken since they left the suite, and neither had he, but they didn't need to. They just wanted this to be over. They wanted to *know*.

It had to be a miscarriage, though. Being the son and brother of doctors, he knew how common they were. Something like twenty percent of first pregnancies, wasn't it? Mom had had one herself, between Connor and Tom. Tom had been six then, and still had a strong memory of the drama of bleeding and tears and a trip to the hospital. The fact that Mom and Dad had had four kids already hadn't made it any less painful, Mom had said to him years later.

Only he didn't believe that. This *had* to be worse, didn't it? To conceive a child together by the most unlikely and miraculous of means, and to marry because of it, only to lose the precious living bond between them after just one day as man and wife.

No. It couldn't be happening. It was too horrible.

He drove erratically. He was lucky it was Sunday morning—there wasn't a lot of traffic. And though he'd lived in Philadelphia all his life, he almost missed the exit and then got the streets confused.

The obstetrician, Dr. Stern, pulled into the parking lot just ahead of them and was opening up when they reached the door.

"Much quicker than the emergency room," he told them, locking the door behind them. "Go straight to the second room on the left and take off your lower clothing, Mrs. Callahan. You'll find a paper sheet. Air-conditioning chills the place down when there's no one here, doesn't it?"

He was a fatherly sort of man, one who exuded experience. Gray hair, glasses, kindly.

In the examining room with Julie, Tom prowled while she undressed. There was a large machine, humming faintly, an ultrasound scanner.

Within a minute, Julie lay flat on a table with a stiff, silly blue sheet draped over her legs and lower torso. She felt calmer now, and safer. The surrounding technology of medicine had taken away some of the primitive, nightmare quality of the morning and put into its place a practical, technical atmosphere that was oddly reassuring.

At least soon they would *know,* and Dr. Stern had obviously been through things like this hundreds of times, which meant that women—couples—survived it and were told what to do next, how to go on living....

Tom took her hand, and they both said at the same time, "Your hand is so cold!"

Then he added painfully, "Oh, hell, Julie."

It was practically all he'd said for the past hour. Hell. And she knew that a large part of it was that he *felt* like hell for having those seconds of doubt and mistrust.

He'd trusted her so little he could have thought *that!* The knowledge ached inside her, beyond the ache of the baby, and made a painful distance between them, even though he was touching her now, pressing her hand in his, sitting as close as he could get.

Suddenly she saw quite clearly the choice she had before her. It was as if the looming threat of losing their baby had put everything into its proper place. She knew she could let Tom's lapse of trust make a huge difference, could turn it into a fat moth of resentment and anger that would nibble away at the fabric of what they had, all the *good* things they'd started to have, until it fell in rotten tatters and there was nothing left.

Or she could let it go. Just let it go.

"Tom?" she said, looking at him.

"Yes? What is it?"

She could see the suffering in his dark eyes. He was leaning toward her, almost hurting her hand. His hair was thick and wild.

"About this morning." It seemed like hours ago. "When you first came in and saw—"

"Oh, Julie." He groaned. "I'd give anything to take back those words. Anything! It was... I was—"

"I know. I know." Her throat hurt. "They're forgotten, Tom. Okay? They're wiped out. I know you were—I mean, people react out of— Just be with me, please?'' Tears came, flowing silently.

''Oh, Julie...'' He kissed the hand that was engulfed in his grip, then bent urgently to touch his mouth to her lips, and as they kissed clumsily with lingering, passionate need, they could both taste the salt.

Then the door opened and Dr. Stern said kindly, ''Now, let's find out what's going on, shall we? Let's put a bit of gel on your abdomen and see what we can see.''

''You mean there may still be a baby?'' Tom demanded, almost harshly, as if he didn't believe it. *Couldn't* believe it.

''Let's take a look,'' Dr. Stern said. ''There are some good signs. I'm not promising.''

The clear gel made a small, cold pool on Julie's stomach, gradually warming to body temperature as the obstetrician spread it out. He brought the probe to her skin, still working beneath the sheet, and slid it slowly back and forth. A confusing series of shapes and textures blurred and distorted themselves on the ultrasound screen until finally he focused on one dark irregular crescent standing out against the gray, grainy background.

''There you go, Mr. and Mrs. Callahan,'' he said softly. ''Inside that crescent. That paler shape. A baby. And there's its heartbeat. Do you see it? That pulsing blur in the center?''

''Yes. Yes, I see it!'' Julie cried. ''Oh, that's... that's...''

"It's the best piece of television I've ever seen!" Tom muttered joyfully.

"And there's something else a little farther..." Dr. Stern mumbled. "Ah!"

Julie was confused, too exultant about that unmistakable sign of life to take in what he said. Here was the irregular crescent again, but the shape looked a little different. Fatter at one end. No, hang on, this was a second crescent, and Dr. Stern gave a gentle crow of triumph when he found the fluttering pulse in the center of the paler gray shape at the crescent's core.

Tom was the first to understand. "Is it— Great balls of— Are you saying it's *twins?*" he asked, his voice hoarse.

"Twins it is," Dr. Stern confirmed, beaming. "Viable, living twins, and their size is right for dates. Congratulations!"

"Twins," Julie echoed in a daze. "Even after all that blood."

"Bleeding in pregnancy is very frightening," the obstetrician agreed. "But it's not necessarily significant. There may have been a tear in one of the placentas, but your body allows for that by building more placental tissue than it needs in the first place."

"Then as long as the bleeding stops, everything's normal?" Tom demanded.

"Normal for twins," Dr. Stern told him. "Which isn't quite the same thing! Take things easy for a while, Mrs. Callahan. I'd like to see you again within the next few days for a proper prenatal workup. And, uh, I'd strongly advise against having marital relations over the next week."

Dr. Stern fixed on both of them in a gaze severe enough to match his name, frowning over the top of his glasses. They nodded silently.

"And now," he continued, "if you'll excuse me for hurrying you along, I'll be needed at the hospital shortly for a delivery."

"No marital relations for a week," Tom repeated faintly.

"Self-control," the doctor suggested heartily. "I'm sure you can do it."

"Oh, yes," Tom agreed. "Of course we can. I mean…"

Julie sat up and saw Tom's suffering glance. Her pupils dilated in shock. Marital relations. The formality and distance of the phrase seemed to conjure up the most incredibly realistic images of the very thing Dr. Stern had forbidden them to do.

"I'll, uh, wait for you outside, Julie," Tom muttered. He coughed as he left the room, trying to clear an annoying catch in his throat, but it wouldn't go.

No marital relations for a week.

He'd always had a stubborn streak. Defiant, even. As a kid, being told he couldn't do something always immediately provoked his determination to go ahead and do that exact thing *twice*.

Even in his late teens, when Mom and Dad had suggested he really *ought* to go to college and learn something concrete about business and computers before plunging headlong into the software design field with Patrick, he'd had the same stubborn response. Stubborn and defiant to the end.

Twelve years later, and he still didn't have a college degree, somewhat to his regret. He'd told Mom and Dad, only half joking, that it was their own fault. If only they hadn't insisted that college was so important!

He had the most overpowering urge to perform the wildest and most shocking set of marital relations since Don Juan and— No. Samson and— Well, he couldn't think of any actually *married* couples who'd attained the sort of sexual extravagance he was envisaging.

But he did want Julie. Wanted his wife naked against him in bed, their breathing fast and urgent, their skin hot and pulsing, their climax aching and earth-shattering and tender and triumphant.

Then it struck him. It wasn't just a week. By the terms of their prenup they weren't supposed to consummate this marriage at all. Ever. He was tempted to blame his lawyers for such a piece of flagrant stupidity, then remembered it had been his own idea.

"Julie, what is it?" Tom breathed, his guts twisting with fear as he lunged toward her hating himself for leaving her, although she'd suggested it.

He had spent the afternoon working at his apartment, and he had just got back to their suite. Julie was watching TV, her feet up on the couch and her body propped against a nest of fat, shiny cushions, sipping a cool drink. When he came in, she burst into tears.

If something was wrong, why hadn't she called? She knew he'd be at the apartment.

She was flapping her hands. "Nothing. It's nothing."

"How can it be nothing? You're sobbing your heart out."

"I'm pregnant."

His tension eased. "Well, yes, I thought we'd already established that pretty thoroughly."

He sat beside her on the couch, his hip against the warm curve of her side.

"No, I mean that's what's making me cry. Hormones. You know. One minute I'm up in the clouds. So happy, Tom, about the babies. And the next—"

"But there must be *something*."

"Happy to see you," she admitted. "Just... missed you, Tom."

"Oh, sweetheart..."

He bent toward her. How could he have done anything else? At first she tasted of her tears, but the salt soon disappeared to leave only the tangy sweetness of the iced juice she'd been drinking. Their mouths were soft against each other to begin with. He felt almost tentative.

If this makes her cry again...

For a moment, he thought it had. He heard little

sounds coming from her throat, but then he realized at once they were mews of pleasure, not sadness or rejection. The thought that she might need this as much as he did set the blood pumping through him.

Her whole body was starting to communicate her desire now. First, she stretched her hands up and clasped them behind his head, making a band of heat against his neck. Then he felt her fingers combing through his hair. He lowered himself to her, and she twisted onto her back so his chest was grazing those incredible breasts. He at once felt the hardening of her nipples into tight little buds that he wanted to caress and suckle.

He brought a hand down to slide beneath the hem of her shirt, then realized it wasn't enough and instead began to tackle the small buttons one by one from the top, until at last he could part the fabric.

Searing his mouth across hers, he pulled away just enough to look at her—the creamy swell of her breasts, so precariously contained. After a whole day of agonizing self-control, he couldn't resist.

He reached inside the shirt and flicked her bra straps down her arms. One, then the other. He was rewarded by exactly what he'd wanted—the sight of her breasts spilling from behind the lace and into his waiting hands.

Julie watched Tom at his task, almost unable to breathe. She shouldn't let this happen and yet was powerless to stop it. There were half a dozen compelling reasons he must not kiss her like this, must not teasingly unbutton her shirt, must absolutely not caress her tender breasts, making her nipples as hard as two knots in a rope.

Must not, but *was,* and she was helpless, barely moving a muscle unless it was to arch against him more strongly, inviting his hands, inviting his mouth.

He bent lower and his lips touched hers again. She responded, parting herself to him and feeling the tease of his tongue against the sensitive lining of her mouth. He trailed his lips down her neck and lower, then brushed each tingling nipple.

"They're so dusky and dark," he whispered, cupping her and tracing his finger around the distinct edge of brown-pink. "I never thought they'd be so dark."

"They didn't used to be. They get darker every day," she answered, set on fire by the intimacy of what he was doing.

No man had ever touched her breasts like this or talked about them with such gentleness and awe.

Tom shuddered, aching with need. He wanted to pick her up and carry her to the bedroom, slide her feverishly out of her clothes and make love to her urgently over and over again. The knowledge that he could not was like a strangling cord around him.

Those newly darkened nipples, which seemed to be demanding his mouth, told the whole story. Her body and the babies it carried were too delicately attached to each other right now.

He knew she wanted it as much as he did. It was as clear in the whole length of her body as it would

have been if she'd used words. The sheen of mois-
ture that glistened on her lips told him. The flush
in her cheeks clamored it, as did the way she was
arching to invite his touch on her sensitive breasts.

But how would she feel if they both gave in to
this and it triggered another bleed, a more powerful
one that tore the fragile tissue completely away?

If they lost the babies now they'd end up blaming
each other, hating each other, and he wasn't prepared to take that risk.

"Julie…"

He had his back to her. Didn't want her to see
what a fight this was.

"I know," she answered huskily. "You don't
have to explain."

He groped for a way to deal with this and came
up with humor.

"Man, I tell you, that damn doctor! He has a lot
to answer for, doesn't he?"

"I know," she said, lightning fast, on the same
track. "The nerve of the man, putting such ideas
into our heads!"

"Never would have thought of anything like this,
but for him."

"Never!"

"Maybe we should switch to someone else on
Adam's list."

"Someone who'd tell us to have marital relations
at least three times a day."

"Six."

"Six times. Even better. Then maybe we wouldn't want to at all."

"Uh, Julie, I think I'll just take a shower at this point."

He turned to face her, very slowly, to give her plenty of warning, and found that she'd finished buttoning her shirt. She must have worked fast, because she'd had to get that bra back in place.

"Go ahead," she nodded. "Please. You first."

"First?"

"There's only one shower, remember?" she pointed out. "So you go first. That's what you wanted, isn't it?"

"I guess it is."

"Only I'm having one, too, so don't use up all the cold water!"

Somehow they managed to get through the night, and he blessed her for having a sense of humor. It beat cold showers any day, and he was in a position to make a studied evaluation of that fact.

Joshing their way through dinner in the hotel's grill bar, and then breakfast the next morning in the atrium garden restaurant, was fun, and for an hour or two at each end of his dream-tossed night's sleep, he almost forgot quite how much he ached.

They checked out of the hotel suite on Monday morning at nine.

Chapter Seven

Real life rolled in with a vengeance, like a summer thunderstorm.

Tom had the morning to help Julie get settled into his apartment, then he needed to get to work. Patrick was clamoring for his time. Julie had planned to jump in the deep end, also. She wanted to send out her résumé to various architectural and design firms, and call the assistant project manager at Case Renfrew who'd promised her some more contract work.

There were some boxes of work-related material to unpack in the apartment. They contained mainly the latest professional journals and magazines, which she was way behind on. They'd been delivered from her apartment the week before last by Marcia.

Somehow, though, she didn't feel like tackling any of it, and anyway none of it seemed to fit under the heading of Dr. Stern's "take things easy."

Tom had questions for her as he was ready to leave after a quick lunch. "Are you going to call the dreaded Dr. Stern's receptionist today, Julie? Make an appointment for your prenatal? And have you told your mom about the twins, yet? Did you call her yesterday from the hotel while I was out?"

"Not yet."

She hadn't told her mom about the pregnancy at all, although she wasn't sure if Tom realized that.

It said something, though, about their strange and not quite real marriage, that her mother's lack of interest was so easy to hide. If she and Tom had known each other better, longer... If they were really, thoroughly in love, he'd have known she had something on her mind.

"I'll call Mom soon," she said lightly. "Tomorrow or Wednesday. I know she's tied up with that movie, you see."

"And I want to call Adam and see how he's doing with Amy," Tom reminded himself. "Oh, and with the prenatal, could you make it for late in the day? After five. Any day except Wednesday, because I have a meeting."

"You mean you want to be there?" she asked.

He froze in the act of putting on his dark suit jacket. She'd only seen him dressed this way once, at the wedding. The effect was devastating. Distancing, too. The expensive, understated suit shouted his success. "Sorry," he said. "I thought you'd want me."

"I do," she answered. "But it's up to you. I know how busy you are, Tom."

"Never too busy for something like that, okay?" he said, his gaze locking on hers. "Never. Remember that!"

For some reason, it sounded almost like a threat.

When he'd gone, the apartment felt too silent, too empty, although her designer's eye had told her when she first saw it last week that it was a charming place. It was part of a big Victorian mansion, subdivided into four, expensively renovated to blend period detail with modern comfort and a clean, elegant line.

The place wasn't huge. A country-style kitchen and two bathrooms. A combination living and dining area. A master bedroom and two more good-size rooms, currently used as a study and a spare room. She'd be sleeping in the spare room. They hadn't discussed this, but she'd noted that it was freshly made up with sheets and comforter in a pattern of tiny dots and wildflowers, which told its own story about what Tom intended.

Either the spare room or the study, they hadn't yet decided which, would be remodeled over the next few months as a nursery. With twins coming, she really wanted the room to work, and planned to design the changes herself.

Maybe a pile of magazines would give her some

ideas, Julie thought, with the first spurt of energy and optimism she'd had all day.

Not a good thing, that little spurt. It gave her another impulse, as well, which ended, perhaps predictably, in disappointment—she called her mom.

And of course she'd forgotten what the time difference would mean.

"Are you crazy, honey? Calling me now?" Those were Sharon Gregory's first shrieked words. "We were on our way out the door, and I only picked up in case it was the studio calling with a change of schedule."

"Sorry, Mom. But I just wanted to—"

"Honey, can I call you back? Of course I want to hear about the wedding and Anthony. Every detail. But for now I'm—"

"Anthony? Who's—"

"Tony, I mean. I assumed it was Anthony."

"Tom. His name's Tom. Not Tony."

"Really? Sexy name. Tom Callahan. Very sellable. But, honey, if we're even *two seconds* late for this—"

"Okay. Sure. Of course."

"I'll call you back as soon as there's any news. Cross your fingers for us, baby."

"I will. But, Mom, I haven't given you my new number at—"

Click. The phone was dropped hastily into its cradle on the other end of the line, and Julie imagined her mother skittering out the door in overly tight clothing, overly high heels and an overly stretched face. She'd had it lifted for the first time last year, while also having her implants enlarged. Five years from now, she would look like she was Julie's younger sister.

The door buzzer sounded moments later, and Julie pressed the intercom. The first thing she heard was a baby crying, followed immediately by Beth Callahan's voice. "May I come up, Julie?"

Julie had rarely been so glad to see someone in her life.

Beth arrived at the top of the polished hardwood stairs and staggered through the door in cheerful confusion. She had baby Amy, still crying, in one arm, a huge diaper bag and a portable infant car seat in the other.

"You can send me away if you're busy," she said, "but not until I've given this squaller a bottle."

Without ceremony or apology, she handed Amy to Julie, opened the diaper bag and began scooping powdered formula into a bottle of sterilized water.

"I'm looking after her during the day until Adam finds a nanny," she explained.

"She's a darling," Julie said, pressing her nose against the silky little head and inhaling the sweet, delicious baby smell. Amy's crying had quieted.

"She is! He'd kill to get some time off work, too," Beth went on. "But this is the last year of his residency, just started, and the hospital system shows no mercy in that area. I guess Tom's feeling the same."

"About the hospital system?" she echoed, raising her voice over the baby, who was losing patience again.

"About killing for time off work. Julie, if you're mad at him about the honeymoon and—"

"I'm not."

"Don't be. He'll do all he can to juggle things. I know him. He's not like my Patrick, who still needs a big jolt before he gets his priorities right."

"Tom's got his right?"

"You think so, don't you?" There came an anxious mother-in-law's look.

"Yes, I do." She nodded, already loving this woman. "Just nice to hear it confirmed by someone who knows, that's all."

"So were you a bit lonely? Or was I wrong?"

"I was a bit lonely," Julie admitted.

Beth shook the bottle, then held it up. "Ready. You can give her back now."

"Yes, or could I..."

"We'll do half each," Beth said firmly, holding out her arms for the frantic infant. "I'm being selfish, I know you want to get in some practice, but she's so precious to me right now, Julie. So very precious."

"Oh, I understand, Beth. I do!"

"I could see what it was doing to Adam to have lost her, you see, and now I almost don't dare to let her go." She sniffed back a tear, tucked the baby into the crook of her arm and began feeding her.

The crying turned into a hiccup, a slurp and a croon, then stopped altogether.

"Now, don't you go too fast, little girl!" Beth said gently. "I know these bottles. They're not quite as good as what nature makes. They let in too many air bubbles."

"I wasn't planning to use a bottle," Julie said. "But I might have to, now, for part of the time, if I can't produce enough milk of my own. We're having twins, Beth."

In hindsight, it wasn't the best way to break the news. Amy certainly didn't think so. She spluttered and cried as Beth accidentally jerked the bottle in her mouth, and wouldn't settle again until she'd been put up on her grandmother's shoulder for a comforting burp.

"Now, run that by me again," Beth said weakly. "You did say twins, right? How did you find out so soon?"

Which, of course, meant worrying her about the bleed.

"I can see you're just like Tom." It was Beth's final verdict on the issue. "You can't just meet, fall in love, get married, get pregnant and have a baby, like ordinary people. You have to meet, fall in love, get pregnant, get married, and have *twins!*"

Even then, she'd got the order all wrong, Julie thought.

I got pregnant first, then we met and got married, and I didn't fall in love until—

Yesterday. Had it happened yesterday? It was

like looking into a camera before getting it into focus. You knew what you were seeing—just a blur and jumble of color, like a dozen different moods— but you didn't know exactly what you were looking at, then suddenly there it all was, as sharp and clear as day, named and waiting for you.

Love.

She loved Tom, with all the completeness and breadth and depth that meant. She loved his body to the point of aching. She loved his tenderness and care. She loved his energy, his humor, his openness and the way he meshed with his big, loving family. She wanted to be in his life forever, as permanently and inextricably as she'd wanted to be in that photo he'd shown her two and a half weeks ago.

She wanted to belong with him. She wanted to belong in his heart. Most of all, she wanted him to feel that way about her.

As she watched Beth Callahan crooning tenderly over her little granddaughter, she was torn between believing it could happen and knowing it couldn't.

How could it? The prenuptial agreement bore witness to their shared caution. It contained forty-seven clauses, reaching forward into an unimaginably distant future when their child or children— yes, the prenup had even allowed for the possibility of twins—reached adulthood.

She thought of how Tom's first instinct had been to distrust her when he'd seen the red stain on her legs. She didn't blame him for it. In his position, she might have thought the same. But it spoke more clearly than words about the gulf that existed between them.

The other thing that had happened yesterday—their overpowering physical hunger for each other—was only a deceptive screen in front of that deeper reality.

"We've just had a call from your husband, Mrs. Callahan," said Dr. Stern's young, redheaded receptionist as Julie gave her name at the front desk for her five-thirty appointment. "You only just missed him. He says he'll be a little late, but go ahead and he'll be here."

"Thanks," said Julie.

She hid her disappointment. It was a small thing. After all, did Tom really need to be here while she answered a barrage of questions on her past medical history? No. But since the babies were the only thing that bound them together, she found herself wanting to grab onto any baby-related business they had, because it meant that they saw each other, and talked, and touched.

Most of the time, Tom was too busy for that. If she hadn't known about the upcoming product launch, she might have thought he was hiding in his work. But from what?

Me. Who am I kidding? It's not just the launch. He is hiding.

He'd been home late the past three nights, bringing dinner for both of them. He'd forbidden her to cook, and he had a maid come in twice a week, so she wasn't exactly enslaved to domestic chores.

After each meal, he'd disappeared into his study to work some more, locked in his chair in front of the bright computer screen for hours as if he was attached to it by an electric cable.

During the day, Julie had been busy with work she could do largely at home for Case Renfrew.

So here they were, a standard-issue professional couple, both with deadlines, leaving each other phone messages with secretaries and notes on the fridge, and they'd known each other three weeks, been married five days and were nine weeks pregnant with twins.

Does that explain why I feel like I'm living in someone else's dream?

She got called in three minutes later, and emerged after nearly half an hour clutching a large folder filled with booklets on pregnancy, hospital routine and birth, pamphlets on prenatal testing and diagnosis and enough coupons offering formula samples and baby lotion samples and diaper samples to feed, anoint and diaper the twins for several weeks.

Tom was there, the middle one of three men, sitting in what looked like the official father-to-be position on a gray leather couch. All three men were perched on the edge of it, looking anxious, like they wanted to go home in case something in the air here was catching.

Tom got up at once, and then he didn't look anything like the other two men anymore. He looked like a big chunk of heaven. He was dressed for his meeting in a power suit of deep charcoal gray. The way it hung emphasized his height. He seemed to fill the waiting room with masculinity and sheer success, but he wasn't conscious of any of that. All his attention was on her.

As soon as he reached her he held out his hands to take hers and bent to brush a kiss across her mouth. "I'm so sorry...."

"Don't worry about it, Tom, I haven't even seen the doctor yet."

He had his arm around her shoulder, and all she wanted to do was lean into it, but he must not guess that, so she stood firmly upright, and soon his arm fell against his side.

"Then what's all this stuff?" he said.

"Goodies from the nurse. Stuff to read about what to expect."

"Let me take it."

"I'm fine."

"I have my briefcase."

He snapped it open, and she handed the crammed folder to him, not wanting to force such an unimportant issue. Maybe it was good that they'd hardly seen each other this week, because when she did see him she just *ached* so badly.

"Okay, Mr. and Mrs. Callahan, Dr. Stern will see you now."

It didn't take long. Apparently everything looked fine.

But as they stood at reception waiting to make another appointment for four weeks away, Tom said to Julie in an undertone, "He didn't mention the thing."

"No. Do you think we should have asked?" Julie didn't stop to wonder how she was so sure what Tom was talking about. The marital relations thing.

"Well, he did say a week," Tom was saying. "And that was on Sunday. I guess I was wondering if he might *extend* it…"

"But he didn't," she came in, "so I guess that means…"

"It's still Sunday."

"Not that it matters, since we're not—"

"Right," Tom agreed quickly. "Not that it matters at all. I was just…you know."

"Concerned," she offered helpfully.

"Yes. That he thinks everything's okay now."

"He seems to."

"So, shall we, uh, stop and eat somewhere? That Italian place where I got the take-out on Monday?"

"Sounds nice."

Although Tom ate an enormous plateful, they didn't stay long over the meal, and he disappeared into his study as soon as they got home.

On Sunday, Patrick and Connor came over for a working brunch. Tom cooked. Scrambled eggs on whole wheat toast, home-fried potatoes, a tangled stack of crisp bacon, juice fresh from a pile of oranges and a huge pot of coffee.

To Julie, it smelled weird and horrible, not like food at all. This particular problem was growing worse, but no one needed to hear about it, least of all Tom. She had no idea he could cook like that, and recognized that it was a spectacular breakfast, even though it held no personal appeal.

"This is a tradition," Connor explained to her, hovering around the bacon like a vulture. "The Callahan working brunch."

"Men think better on a full stomach," Patrick added.

Julie didn't quite trust Patrick. Or didn't feel that he trusted her. He had a reputation as the cynic of the family. *Cynic or womanizer?* Julie wondered. There'd been a few hints.

"And women don't?" She challenged Patrick's comment.

He conceded her point with an irritable shrug, and Tom shot him a quick glance.

"Have you just ditched another babe, Pat?"

"You mean have I ended a relationship with a female friend?" Patrick corrected sourly.

"No, I mean have you ditched a babe. That's how it needs to be phrased in your case."

"Why?"

"Because," Connor told him cheerfully, "you invariably pick women who will confirm every prejudice you already have about the female sex."

"Do we need to have this conversation in front of a member of it?"

"Julie's your sister-in-law now," Connor said. "She needs to know the terrible truth."

"Which is?"

"You don't *want* to trust women."

"And why would that be?"

"Because it's easier to hang on to our beliefs than to challenge them, Pat," Tom said patiently.

"I don't want to discuss this."

"I know," Tom agreed. "So eat up. I just feel sorry for the woman, that's all."

"Which one?"

"The one you ditched."

"I didn't. We came to a mutual parting of the ways."

"Ah! You mean she decided to go back to her husband?"

"Tom, can we quit the character assassination and start assassinating this packaging instead?" Patrick tossed the mock-up of the new software box onto the table as if several splashes of juice and egg spilled on it wouldn't matter.

"Now tell me why I hate it," he demanded.

"It's the colors," Julie said, then explained what she meant. They thrashed through the issue for two hours, then decided to tell their art department to throw out the mock-up and start again, although the deadline would be critically tight.

"Keep her," said Patrick to Tom at the door as he and Connor were leaving.

He and Tom glanced at Julie, just visible through the kitchen door. She was loading the dishwasher.

Tom had forbidden it, but she'd pointed out, "I'll grow roots if I keep lying around like I've been doing. Probably branches and leaves and a big old tire swing as well. Let me, Tom. I feel fine, and it's a full week now since— Well, since Dr. Stern told us what he told us…about the thing."

"Keep her?" Tom echoed with a catch in his throat. "Do you think I'm not planning to?"

He was hedging. Patrick, of all people, didn't need to know about their prenup, with its cynical assumption of an inevitable divorce.

"He means it as a threat," Connor said helpfully. "Fair warning of his intentions, Tom. If you show any sign of letting her go, he'll poach."

"Connor, keep at least a thread of good taste in your jokes," Patrick growled.

"Who says I was joking?"

"I do! And I mean it, Tom, in the spirit of brotherly love. You've done well for yourself."

"Thanks," he answered, then added without thinking, "I'm starting to think so, too."

"*Starting* to?" Connor challenged.

Tom didn't even try to dig himself out of *that* hole. Let his brothers think what they liked! Right now, all he wanted was for them to get the heck out of here so he could have Julie to himself and…

And what? Break that very expensively drafted prenup into a thousand tiny pieces?

Yes! Damn it, *yes!* He actually *ached* as he had ached for the past two hours, for the past week, with the effort of trying to think about anything else.

But when the door closed on his brothers half a minute later, he hesitated in the hallway for longer than he'd have thought possible. Was this fair to Julie? Was it even remotely what she wanted?

Chapter Eight

"Tom?"

He heard her tentative question and looked up to meet her worried stare. Hardly surprising she looked that way. He wasn't in the habit of standing at his own front door for minutes on end like this. He had his forehead pressed hard against the unyielding wood and his forearm resting crossways above it, supporting his leaning weight. He had no idea exactly how long he'd been standing like this. Glancing past her, he saw that the round table in the big kitchen where they'd eaten was spotless.

"What is it, Tom?" she demanded urgently, coming toward him.

"Nothing. I'm fine."

She wasn't buying it. "Something to do with the software?" she pressed. "Another problem?"

"No. I'm fine."

"Strange expression on your face for someone who's fine."

Maybe if she hadn't kept coming forward. Maybe if she hadn't touched him, laid those warm fingers across his arm, with that little tuck of a frown between her brows, and her wide mouth so soft and straight and serious.

"Julie, don't do this."

She froze. "Do what?"

"Nothing. It's not your fault."

"What's not my fault?"

"Nothing. Absolutely nothing."

"Tom?" Even the way she said his name, leaving her lips parted at the end of it, made his body sing.

"It's just…" The words tore out of him. He shouldn't say them. But he had to. "It's a week since that scary time at Dr. Stern's office. All I can think of is that if this was a normal marriage, if we didn't have that prenup, I'd be allowed to…it'd be safe to make love to you now. And at the moment that's the *only* thing in the *universe* I want to do. So when you touch me I just wonder how I'm going to find it in me to resist."

Her hand dropped like a snake after a strike. It was almost funny. Last week, for a while, she'd seemed to share his need. He remembered that little talk they'd had about cold showers. Evidently she didn't feel that way now.

He'd stayed away from her as much as possible all week.

It hadn't worked for him, but maybe it had done the trick for her. In theory, this should make resisting her a whole lot easier for him, so why wasn't he feeling happier about it?

Because you want to sleep with her and you can't think beyond that.

He was so consumed with fighting it that he almost didn't take in what she'd said.

"Don't ask me to help you, Tom. Please! Because I've got no help to spare. I'm fighting as hard as you are."

Their eyes met. Seconds later, with desperate urgency, their mouths did the same.

Julie was shaking. She hadn't known until he'd admitted it that he was still feeling this way. Maybe because she hadn't been able to see beyond the power of her need. Now there was no going back. She knew it as surely as she knew her own name.

Julie Callahan.

His kiss was so tender and at the same time so hungry. With his palms pressed into the heavy oak door on either side of her shoulders, he was imprisoning her like a teenager who might hear his new love's parents on the stairs at any moment and had to get in while he could. As his mouth tasted her frantically, his hair tickled her forehead and his chest nudged hard against her sensitive breasts.

Maybe she should have resented his impatience,

but she didn't. It seemed like they'd both waited for so long. So long. Parting her lips, she felt his tongue with hers. Her strength began to drain into the floor, swept away by the power of their need for each other. Fighting to stay on her feet, she reached for him, clamping her hands against his hips and gripping him as his thighs pressed against hers.

"I guess...my bedroom's...a lot more comfortable than this," he finally said, but she couldn't bear to let him go while they covered the endless distance to his room, so she grabbed his shoulders and pulled him to her once more.

He groaned in response to her moment of domination.

They made the move to his bed in stages, stopping every few steps to kiss and hold each other as if more than a second apart might break the spell.

His bedroom windows were shaded by slatted wooden shutters, tilted half open to let in the bright noon light of the summer day, and his bed was unmade. They fell onto it together. Or maybe Tom pulled her down, because she was the one that ended on top, with his warm weight beneath her and his teak-brown eyes looking into hers.

Nothing mattered but their bodies, inflamed and finally joined. He didn't bother with the buttons on her V-necked cotton cardigan, just pulled the garment over her head and then groaned at the sight of her breasts encased in black lace, and the slight, rounded swell of her stomach where the muscles of her lower abdomen had begun to loosen their weave.

The black lace was soon gone. She was equally impatient for his nakedness, and when they finally touched length to length and skin to skin, it felt like coming home.

"Is this really the first time?" he whispered. "Every time I've thought of this with you—and, hell, I've thought of it so often!—it's felt like we must already know each other this way. So familiar. So right."

"I know. I know, Tom."

Neither of them spoke for a long time, and when they settled slowly back to earth, they both fell asleep, with Tom's hair tickling her shoulder and his hand cupping her breast.

She was the one to awaken first, after about an hour. When she slowly opened her eyes and looked down to find his strong forearm lying across her stomach and the swell of her breast overflowing his warm hand, the intimacy of it almost made her cry. *I belong here. I belong with him. I've never belonged like this before.*

He was still fast asleep, his dark lashes feathering against his cheeks and the corners of his mouth tucked up in a tiny smile. She watched him, taking a greedy pleasure in counting all the things about him that she loved. With the urgency of their love-making past, she could admit that his gorgeous male body was not even at the top of her list. It was just *him*.

His family, too. Who else but Tom could have joshed Patrick into throwing off his cynical mood this morning the way he had? She was no longer afraid of Patrick as she had been. Soon he'd be another Callahan for her to love, the way she was starting to love Adam and Liam and Jim and Beth.

Beth. The kind of mother she'd always wanted. A mother who embraced her role, filled it and gloried in it, not one who kept trying to pretend she wasn't a mother at all.

Except maybe I'm being unfair, Julie decided. *I haven't given Mom a chance. I haven't even told her about the babies yet, and she was so distracted last week she didn't even wait to hear my new phone number.*

Suddenly, she really wanted to reach out and bridge the distance. She felt bad that she'd been so close to switching all her love and loyalty to Beth Callahan.

Tom was still dead to the world. He'd worked till past midnight every night this week, and had risen before six. She'd heard him a couple of times in the middle of the night, too, prowling. He must have been exhausted, and now his body was letting go.

When she gently eased his hand away from her breast, leaving it bereft and cold, she was able to

slide across the bed and out from beneath the crookedly draped sheet without making him stir.

Silently, she dressed, feeling the echo of his
touch again in the cups of her lacy bra, the cool
weight of the cotton cardigan on her skin and the
soft drape of her flared pants. He hadn't moved or
woken. If he had, she'd have shamelessly crawled
onto the bed again to snuggle against him.

In the living room, she picked up the phone and
dialed her mother's number, not planning how
she'd make the announcement about the twins, desperately hoping they'd have the opportunity to really talk this time.

After three rings, the phone was picked up.

"Mom?"

"Julie? Honey, I can't *believe* you haven't
called! I didn't have your number!"

"I know. I'm sorry. Can we talk now?"

"Talk? I could cry! He *didn't get* it, Julie! They
got another draft of the script and the character's
been written out completely. Can you imagine? Not
an inkling to us."

"People say it's a cruel profession. Is it time he
maybe tried something else, after fifteen years?"

"You just don't understand, do you?"

"I guess not. But, Mom, I have some news that
might cheer you up a little."

"Really, honey?" She sounded doubtful.

"Tom and I… Well, we're expecting twins next
February."

"Oh, dear Lord, you poor thing!"

"What?"

Her shock came through loud and clear, and Sharon Gregory backtracked fast.

"Honey, I mean, it's great if you're happy, of course it is," she said. "But you'll never get your figure back the way it was. You know that, don't you? One baby is bad enough."

"I'm not exactly thinking much about my figure right now." Julie fought to keep the anger out of her voice. "I had a bit of trouble last week, but it seems to have settled now, and all I'm thinking of, and Tom, is that we hope everything is okay."

"Trouble? You mean losing the pregnancy?"

"Yes. It was—"

"A lot of women miscarry, especially twins."

"I know, which is why—"

"Honey, this is going to sound callous, but believe me, I'm only thinking of you. If it *does* happen, think of it as a blessing. Obviously it's why you got married, because you were pregnant. I thought it all sounded suspiciously sudden! But it's a terrible way to start a marriage. If nature gives you a way to wipe the slate clean and start over, then take it and be grateful, okay? I'm sure Thomas will be. I'm sure you didn't do it on purpose, but it's a terrible thing to put on a man, getting pregnant to him, taking his freedom before he's ready."

There was a clatter at the other end of the phone, and then Matt's voice, sounding muffled.

"Matt, darling, is that you?" Sharon said, her hand only partially covering the receiver. "Cindy called earlier and wants us to go to lunch." There was a short pause and another voice in the background, then, "No, this isn't Cindy now. This is Julie. She's miscarrying twins, poor sweetheart." Another muffled clatter, then her voice sounded clearly again. "Honey, I probably should go."

"I'll give you my new number," Julie said, through a tight throat.

"Hang on. Where's a pen? Okay, shoot!"

Half a minute later, Julie put down the phone. Physically, she and her mom were almost a continent apart. Emotionally, it felt like even farther.

My babies, our babies, are more important than Matt's movie and my figure and Tom's freedom. I know I'm not wrong to feel that way! I won't lose them. I can't!

She hadn't thought of it this way before, but there was one very important sense in which her mom was right. Her talk of wiping the slate clean, starting over. If the babies miscarried, then the whole reason for Julie's marriage to Tom fell apart.

I couldn't bear it, to lose all three of them, Tom and the babies, like that.

At the stark knowledge, on top of the painfully disappointing phone call with her mother, she perched, frozen, on the edge of Tom's natural leather couch, staring into nothing, until a movement in the bedroom doorway told her that he was awake and watching her.

She forced a smile. It felt like biting on a knife blade. Then she saw the lazy grin fade from his face.

"What's up?" he said.

"Nothing. I'm fine," she lied. She didn't want him to guess what she was thinking and feeling. "But how about you?" she added quickly. "You must have been tired. You slept for quite a while."

"Tends to happen if I'm real, *real* relaxed," he replied, unashamed of the open hint about what had got him into that condition.

"I guess so," she agreed, as if he'd said that he thought cornflakes went better with milk.

"You're dressed," he noticed. "You've been awake for a while, then."

"I didn't really sleep," she lied again. "I was pretty restless. I've been reading."

She waved at the coffee table, where luckily there was a magazine.

Though she hadn't yet fully thought it through, she knew it was crucial not to have him guess how powerfully she'd been stirred by their lovemaking. He mustn't think it was special. He mustn't know she'd fallen more deeply in love with him than ever, while lying in his arms. And he absolutely mustn't realize how much she ached to reach that ecstatic height with him again and again.

She didn't understand why she felt all this so

strongly until an hour later, when she went to the bathroom and found blood in her panties again. Just a smear, this time, but it was enough to panic her. Tom had gone out for milk and the newspaper a couple of minutes ago, and she was glad. She didn't want to tell him about the latest episode, nor about calling Dr. Stern. Somehow that would make it more real, more frightening.Because the doctor had suggested abstaining from marital relations until she reached the second trimester.

Last week, at some level, it had been funny. Such a serious and rather coy expression for what she and Tom had just done. It wasn't funny anymore.

We mustn't make love again. We never should have in the first place. Oh, I wanted it. I still do. But if making love means I lose the babies, then I'll lose Tom, as well, and I can't lose Tom!

Nor could she tell him any of this. What would he think if he knew how deeply she had fallen for him? Even when he'd talked about the possibility that their marriage might strengthen and be a success, he'd never mentioned love, just respect and trust and staying together for the sake of their child.

Respect and trust. Those were such dry, impossible names for what she felt, the way ''marital relations'' was a dry, impossible way to describe the happiness and total fulfillment she'd felt with Tom in his bed.

There was a twisted irony in all of this. To have

a chance of keeping him in her heart and in her life, she had to pretend she didn't want him at all.

She'd faked it.

That was the only answer Tom could come up with as to why Julie had switched off the way she had. He hadn't really wanted the newspaper, and he'd deliberately downed the last of the milk, straight from the carton, so he'd have the excuse to go for more.

Heading into the nearest convenience store, not caring what anyone thought of his scowling face, he couldn't believe how differently he felt now compared to how he'd felt an hour ago. He'd woken in a bed that was still rumpled from their lovemaking. It still held her sweet, intoxicating scent. Still felt gloriously warm. He'd stretched, enjoying his male nakedness, hoping she'd be back in a minute so he could hold her, discover her again with his hands and his mouth.

When she hadn't appeared, he'd dressed quickly and carelessly in jeans and an old T-shirt to go look for her. He wanted to touch her, caress her, not necessarily because he wanted to coax her into bed again right away, but just because she was so beautiful.

She was filling his heart to overflowing these days, and he didn't know what to make of this. He was a little scared to think about it, actually. Loretta had burned him so badly he didn't even know if he believed in the word love when it came to his own life. He wasn't sure that he ever wanted to give a feeling that name again.

Too dangerous. He didn't want to be that vulnerable.

Perhaps he was more like Patrick than he wanted to admit.

He'd told himself to stop wondering, stop doubting, and just *go* to her, *take* her, and then, standing in the doorway with a goofy, love-struck kind of a grin on his face, he'd seen her frozen on the couch, looking miserable and tight and desperate and about a million miles away from his own state of relaxation and fulfillment.

And when he'd tried to find out what was wrong, she'd lied.

He could only assume that she'd lied through the whole of that sizzling, sensual encounter. During the white-hot intensity of their shared climax, he'd have sworn on his life that Julie was as caught up in it as he was. She'd showed a passion and total involvement he'd never imagined in a woman. But what explanation could there be for the way she'd turned off so quickly afterward?

Only that she hadn't been caught up in it at all.

He didn't know whether to be angry or to despise himself. Was he that lacking in sensitivity to a woman's needs and feelings?

No, to *Julie's* needs and feelings. He didn't give a damn about women in general! Right now, *she* was the only one who mattered, and he hoped it would stay that way.

They *had* to talk about this when he got home.

She wouldn't, though. She just would not, and she was as cunning and slippery as an eel about it. Since when was she this deceitful? One of the things he most liked about her was how fresh and open and true she was.

But when he got home, she was cooking something elaborate, which required total attention in case the sauce curdled or something, and, by the way, Patrick had called. "And your mother, and someone called Zeke. He said you'd know the number."

She gave the information immediately, in a big rush, as if it relieved her enormously that she was able to say it.

"When?" he growled, raking his suspicious gaze over that blond head, bent over the skillet.

"Oh, just a few minutes ago, all three calls, one on top of the other. It's all written down," she said eagerly, looking up at last to throw him a dazzling, desperate smile. What was she doing? Going for secretary of the month?

"Julie…"

"Patrick said it was urgent. He told me the only point of Sunday, in his opinion, is to get a head start on the rest of the week."

"Right. He would," Tom growled. "Okay, I'll call him."

"And—"

"I know. Zeke Butterfield and Mom."

"She and I had a good talk."

"Right."

He shot her a suspicious glance. The third in the past thirty seconds. What was *that* in her tone, suddenly? A word he hadn't even known was in his vocabulary—wistfulness. She sounded wistful. What the hell was she thinking?

Weeks passed, and he still didn't know.

Chapter Nine

"Warning—this marriage has been declared a disaster zone," Tom muttered under his breath.

He'd come into the apartment at six in the evening and, as usual, found it empty.

It was early October. The steam of summer was gone, and the scents of fall filled the air—smoke and cold. Well, cold wasn't exactly a scent, he amended. More of a feeling. One he didn't like at the moment.

Julie was halfway through her pregnancy with no further problems. After some frantic weeks, the software launch had come and gone. The product was selling better than forecast. Profits were rising. The glitches in the new game, which they hoped would hit the stores early next year, were being ironed out one by one. All fine and dandy. The hell of it was, none of it mattered a damn.

Correction. Julie and the babies mattered, to the point where finding her out of the apartment when he got home from work each day tied his gut instantly in knots and had his mind sifting through half a dozen scenarios, each more appalling and unlikely than the last.

He shouldn't think this way. She'd given him no reason to. But he knew that everything about their marriage was so fragile, from the pregnancy to the paper on which their marriage certificate was printed. Their prenup was probably the strongest thing in their shared lives, and even that had been broken.

Just once.

In two and a half months, they hadn't repeated *that* mistake, thank goodness, though his body crawled with wanting to every single day.

Restless and dissatisfied, he went into the new nursery. Since they were having twins, they'd chosen the biggest of the other rooms to be done over for the babies. This happened to be his study, which meant he'd moved his desk and computer into the spare room, which meant he couldn't work at night if Julie wanted to go to bed before him, which she very often did.

In the end, they'd agreed on the only sensible solution. He'd taken the bed in the study and she'd taken the master bedroom, though he still kept his clothes there.

He looked around the nursery to see if anything had changed. It was one of the few subjects on which they communicated well these days. Maybe because it was easy. He loved what she was doing in this room, and she poured her soul into it.

The airy, high-ceilinged room smelled of fresh paint. He went to the windows and pulled them up, as Julie had been doing whenever possible, to let in the crisp fall air and chase out the fumes, then he heard her key in the front door and called out to her, "Julie, is that you?"

Of course it was. He knew the rhythm of her walk by heart.

"Hi."

She came straight into the nursery, lugging two brown paper shopping bags. Below her stretchy pale gray maternity dress, her legs were as long and lean as ever, and she still moved gracefully despite the taut and growing roundness of her belly. He felt a hot surge of desire for her, tangled with currents of protectiveness and very male pride. She looked so beautiful, nurturing their babies.

He watched her arranging the antique blocks she'd pulled out of the shopping bags as if her life depended on getting them neat, piling them into a pyramid, each block precisely aligned and the colors forming a repeating pattern of red, yellow and blue.

Suddenly, and with no logic, he was angry about how much time she was spending on this room. No matter what happened in the future, wouldn't it be better for the twins *now* if he and Julie spent more time with each other?

He almost said something, almost yelled at her, in fact, but managed to stop himself in time. Her wheat-blond hair was screening her face like a curtain, as if all she needed was to focus on arranging the blocks and as if she was so intent on what she was doing that the outside world didn't exist at all.

But then he saw something splash onto the back of her hand. He saw that the hand was shaking, and that she wasn't really thinking about the blocks. She was doing it all mechanically, her designer's eye so acute that she couldn't help doing it perfectly.

For some reason, she was crying, though she was fighting like anything not to, and not to let him see. He didn't dare challenge her about it. He'd asked her innumerable times over the past two and a half months if anything was wrong, if anything was on her mind, and she'd always, always denied it.

He wasn't going to go down that arid, pointless road again.

But he *was* going to take some action. He'd let too much time go by already.

"Julie, are you working tomorrow?"

"I was planning to, yes," she answered him. "I have a few last details to finalize on Mrs. Renfrew's new place."

But it was almost finished now, so she could easily take the next day off. If Tom wanted her to.

Be honest! If Tom wanted her to, she'd take the next ten days off, whether it was easy or not!

Still, she hedged. "Didn't your mom and dad want us to go to a family barbecue on the weekend?"

"I know, but they're my parents," he replied shortly. "They have to put up with it when I blow them off."

"They do?" She loved his parents, loved Tom's easy relationship with them, and had noted that usually he was very considerate of their time.

"This time, they do," Tom growled.

"It's important, then…"

Not strictly.

Not for any reason he could explain.

"Well," he said, "it's Columbus Day weekend coming up. I need to get the lake house winterized. I thought we could drive up there tomorrow, make a four-day weekend of it. I heard a forecast in the car on the way home. They're predicting bad weather for next week, but this weekend's supposed to be sunny."

"I thought Don winterized the house." She frowned.

"He would. Obviously. But it's something I've always preferred to do myself," Tom said firmly, creating a long-running tradition, in the space of eight words, for a house that had only been built for two years. "And we've been so busy, we haven't gotten up there all summer."

Although he knew that if their marriage had been running more smoothly, he would have found the time somehow, even if it meant taking work up there. At the beginning of summer, he'd intended to be there a lot.

"Not since those days in early July," he went on. "Before our wedding. We need a break."

Julie knew that the last thing in the world she needed was to spend four days and, even worse, four nights alone with Tom in the gorgeous wild mountains of upstate New York, but she couldn't say no. It was the *we* that did it when he could so easily have said *I*.

Feeling like she was opening up her chest and showing him her heart, Julie told him, "I'd love to go up to the lake with you tomorrow. You're right. We *do* need a break."

They left at nine the next morning. At the wheel, Tom tried to focus on his driving, but the traffic was light and the road was dry and clear, and there just wasn't a lot of brainpower required for steering.

He wasn't sure, anymore, what he wanted out of this weekend. Or maybe he *was* sure, but it seemed like such an unreachable goal that he didn't even dare to dream it, let alone think of a practical plan for getting there.

Beside him in the passenger seat, Julie was sleeping. She'd reclined the seat back and bundled her navy blue coat into a pillow. Her hair was falling across her cheek.

He couldn't help pretending to himself that they were just like any married couple who were deeply in love. Pretending that when he stopped the car and she stirred, he'd lean over and wake her with a soft kiss on that wide pink mouth. And when they reached the house the first thing they'd do, before they even unpacked, would be to open the heavy drapes in his bedroom and let the afternoon sun fall onto the bed while they made love. And then... And then...

After ten minutes of it, he was angry. At himself. Since when had he been the type to dream? Since never! Dreams were only fuel. You didn't keep them hoarded away like something precious. You used them to drive you on until the dreams became reality. He wasn't going to let Julie go without a fight. He was going to do everything he could to keep hold of this marriage and make it real.

Come Monday, Julie wouldn't know what had hit her.

Pulling up at the dock on the shore of Diamond Lake half an hour later, he gently shook her awake, promising himself that he would kiss her today but planning to save it for later. Just looking at her mouth made it so tempting to change the plan, but he managed to resist.

"Here already?" she said groggily.

He grinned. "I love the way you sleep. Like a bear in winter."

"I know. More in the past four months than in my whole life put together."

"Didn't know I was marrying such a lazy woman."

"Lazy? Hey, I'm making bones and brain cells while I'm asleep! A double set of them! Let me know when *you* learn how to do that!"

"As I said. Like a bear. Even when you wake up. A bear with a sore head."

She laughed. "And you know, there's something else about bears when they wake up after a long sleep."

"I know. They're hungry. Don't worry, I called Barbara last night and asked her to stock the fridge and the pantry."

Tom's parents had spent two weeks here, and several of his younger brothers had brought friends up for weekends, so his housekeeper had been kept busy, as had Don.

Don was here to greet them, about to ferry a load of winter firewood across in the Sportsman. He had his flannel shirtsleeves rolled past the elbows, but the crisp air was quite cold, and Julie was happy to bundle up in her big coat.

"How's the wood coming?" Tom asked his maintenance man.

"This is the last load. You want the furnace started up, as well?"

"I'll handle it," Tom said. "And I'll help you unload."

He started the Riviera and loaded their weekend gear into it. Don was already halfway across the lake in the Sportsman, which was riding low and slow in the water under the weight of the wood. They'd almost caught up to him by the time he reached the island.

"Motor doesn't like the hard work," he said to Tom. "I'd better take a look at it, I think."

"It can wait, Don," Tom answered. "You can get on home as soon as we unload."

He tried to make it sound casual, but inside he was aware of his impatience. He didn't want Don putzing around with the motor all afternoon, calling him out to the shed by the dock to hear a report on progress. Tom could hear for himself that the motor wasn't quite running sweet, but a tune-up could wait a few days.

Meanwhile, he wanted to be alone with Julie as soon as he decently could.

He practically ran up the stairs with their bags and flung Julie some quick instructions about where to find things for a snack.

"Not for me," he told her, then went straight back down to Don at the dock to help him chuck each sawn log onto the wagon that hooked to the back of the ride-on mower.

Half an hour later, Don was at the wheel of the

Riviera heading to the public dock, where his pickup was parked in the sun.

"Now." Tom turned to Julie, his face alight with satisfaction. "The house was cold, wasn't it?"

"Freezing!"

"I'll get the furnace lit, then, and you set a fire for later. Can you manage that? Down on your knees?"

"I'd better be able to, at less than five months!"

"But *can* you?"

"I'll be fine, Tom," she promised him.

"Then we'll take a walk on the island before the sun goes and do some bird-watching."

"Bird-watching? I didn't know you were interested in birds."

He shrugged and grinned. "I'm not. But it makes a useful excuse."

He disappeared into the basement before she could challenge him. An excuse for what?

Surely she had to be imagining that tiny lick of sexual tension in the air, like a small, silent flame. It was only because they were really alone now, in a way they hadn't been since before their wedding. No family, no work commitments, no busy city around them, where it was always too easy to find ways to escape.

And she remembered, also, how elemental their first meeting had been, here alone on an island in the summer heat. The revelations and decisions they'd had to make that day had stripped away all the places on the surface of life where two people could hide from each other. Neither of them had been able to hide that first day, that first week, and now they were back, alone on an island in the crisp display of fall.

It hit her that what Tom had said yesterday about wanting to winterize the house was, like the bird-watching, nothing but an excuse. Even what he'd said about needing a break. There was more to it than that.

He had something planned. She was sure of it. Something he wanted to say.

Divorce.

No! I don't know it's divorce he wants to talk about. She knelt in front of the fireplace and reached for some birch logs, their curved, silvery bark sides fitting cold and smooth into her hands. But she was shaking so much when she set them in the fireplace that the whole heap collapsed, kindling and paper and all, and she had to start again.

She forced herself to concentrate and did such a good job of it that she didn't notice Tom had entered until she'd laid the last log and he said, just behind her, "I can tell you got a few camping badges at Girl Scouts. That's straight out of the manual."

"Startle me like that again and I'll have to start over," she threatened, not bothering to tell him she'd already had to do just that, on his account. "Shall we light it now?"

"Not yet," he suggested. "I've got the furnace lit and it'll start to warm the place. Let's get some air while the sun's still bright. We can light the fire at dusk. Barbara has left us the makings for fondue."

"Fondue!" She couldn't help sounding startled. Fondue by firelight. Dipping twin forks into one big pool of tangy cheese. Food to divorce by?

"You don't like fondue?"

"No, I— That is, yes, I *do* like fondue."

"You can be honest, Julie. If I chuck it in the garbage, Barbara will never know. I guess she thought it'd be romantic, fondue by the fire. It was probably *the* big seduction food when she was courting. She's left a bottle of nonalcoholic champagne, too, and some after-dinner mints. She's cute."

Of course. This was all his housekeeper's idea. "No, it sounds great!" she made herself say. It came out high and unconvincing.

"Listen," he insisted tightly. "I don't give a damn, okay? There's probably some microwave meals in the freezer."

He took a pace toward her, and she began to get up, not as easy a movement as it used to be. She held her growing stomach with one hand, then massaged her lower back with the other when she reached a standing position, arching a little to stretch her cramped muscles. Tom was right in front of her, still speaking, his eyes ablaze.

"Just stop playing it safe, okay, Julie? Stop telling me what you think I want to hear!"

"About fondue?"

"Damn it, about *everything!* But start with fondue. Get in some practice. Do you like Barbara's romantic fantasy for us? Or not?"

"I like it," she said, not looking at him, picking at her fingernails. "I like it, Tom."

"Good," he growled. He didn't sound happy, but then neither had she. "And now I really need some sun and air," he added, turning to lope toward the front door. He made it sound like *she* was responsible for the cold and slightly stuffy atmosphere inside the house.

She followed him, feeling angry. So whose fault was it that fondue had suddenly turned into a big deal?

Mine. Because I thought it was his idea, not Barbara Foster's.

She fought to find something better between them. Humor. During some of their very worst moments, humor had helped. "So where are my binoculars, Tom?" she called after him, trying to catch up.

"Binoculars?"

"Yes! Quick! I think I see a rare Crested Greerson's Puffer Belly."

"I already told you, bird-watching was just an excuse."

"An excuse for what, Tom?" Julie asked softly.

"Just for being with you," he answered. "Why won't you let our marriage grow?"

One arm came around her, while his other hand reached for her face. She felt his warm palm running along her cheek and jawline, then he nudged her chin up, forcing her to meet his eyes. "*Why,* Julie?"

She didn't dare to give him an answer that wasn't honest. She didn't even want to. "Because I'm scared."

"Of losing the babies?"

"Of losing everything."

"What do you mean 'everything?' How could you lose everything? What *is* everything, to you?"

She tried to find the way to say what she felt about him and his family and her sense of belonging, her sense that her whole life was *richer* now, by so much. But she couldn't say it. Couldn't strip herself bare like that. She dropped her gaze, not wanting him to read it all in her face.

He must have read *something,* though. The wrong thing. At that moment she really began to believe in telepathy, because out of everything she'd been thinking, he seemed to snatch that one word out of her thoughts, "richer."

"Oh." His brow cleared, then darkened. "You mean my money. Isn't that taken care of to your satisfaction in the prenup?"

"No, Tom! *Not* that! You mean, still, after more than three months, you think I'm like my cousin?"

She pulled away from him and headed beneath the trees, picking her way awkwardly across the rocks and slippery tawny-brown needles, tears of hurt and frustration drowning her vision.

"Then what?" he demanded, almost shouting, coming after her, catching up quickly. "If it's *not* that, then tell me!"

She shouldn't have looked at him. She should have stopped, steadied herself. But she didn't. And the pine needles were slippery.

She fell.

Not hard. Not against a rock. But the fall shocked and jarred her, and she lay on her side for several seconds, her arm flung over her face, breathing hard and willing the panicky beat of her heart to settle and the hot wash of shock to subside.

Tom reached her. "Julie! Hell..." His voice cracked.

"I'm okay."

"You're talking. That's a start."

He sounded shaky, and his humor, like hers a few minutes earlier, was forced. He dropped beside her and gathered her shaken body into his arms. "Were you trying to give me a scare?"

"I thought your heart probably needed a work-out."

"Thanks for your concern! Are you really all right?"

"Shaky. Can we go back to the house?"

"This second. I'll carry you."

She laughed. "I can walk. Really. Just hold onto me, okay?"

"I'd never let you go. Believe that, Julie."

She didn't answer. He couldn't mean it the way she wanted him to. He was talking about her fall and the babies, not about the rest of their lives. Still, she accepted what he was offering as a precious gift. They walked to the house in a tight, heavy tangle of arms, her cheek pressed against his chest so hard that she could hear the pounding of his heart.

Chapter Ten

He didn't speak until they reached the house, and neither did she. In the southwest, the sun was skimming the tops of the pines. The shadows were getting longer and colder every minute. Tom stopped in the middle of the last finger of sunshine that reached the porch and gathered her even more closely against him, looking into her upturned face.

"Tell me! Is there any pain? You're really not hurt?"

"I'm fine. Might even start breathing again sometime in the next couple of hours. Thanks for... for holding me."

The sun faded like a stage light dimming, and they both looked at the slope of pines beyond the lake. There was just a faint glimmer of gold showing between the dense branches, and the last illusion of warmth was gone.

"You can let me go, now," Julie said.

Slowly, he did.

Inside, the furnace had begun to warm the air, but he went straight to the fire she had laid and lit it, touching the match to the paper in several places. Within seconds the flames had begun to creep rapidly toward the kindling. Then he pulled two chairs close, and Julie sat down.

Soon the wood was cracking and hissing, and she was so absorbed in holding her hands out to bask in the rising heat that she didn't at first notice Tom was no longer in the room.

A couple of minutes later, she heard the microwave ping, and he came back with two steaming mugs of hot chocolate.

"Hot chocolate by the fire in October?" she teased. "What does that leave us for January?"

"Mulled wine and roasted chestnuts?"

"I've never tried either."

"Same here. We'll make a date for it, shall we? Presidents' Weekend? Up here? You bring the chestnuts, I'll bring the wine."

They both laughed, looked at each other, then looked quickly into the fire.

There was a lot to see in a fire. They were still looking at it an hour later, with the last of the fondue still warm in the bottom of the earthenware pot and the bottle of apple-tanged champagne half empty on the hearth. They hadn't talked much. Just more light, silly stuff about the meal.

This time when he spoke, his tone was different.

"I had no right to say what I did about the money back there, Julie." His voice was husky. "I don't know why it came out. That's no excuse. I guess... I know there's so much you don't tell me about what you think and feel. You've seen my family, you know how we are with each other. We don't bottle things up. Because there are so many of us, I guess. Mom and Dad didn't have time to spend hours extracting our emotional secrets. They had to get yanked from us quickly, like pulling teeth or something. But it must have been different for you. You've been an only child all your life. I shouldn't expect great slabs of blunt honesty like I get from those damn brothers of mine."

She gave him a quick, intense glance. He was leaning forward, perched at the edge of his chair, with his forearms on his knees, not just looking at the fire but *staring* at it, frowning and jiggling his fondue fork in his hand.

And she loved him so much the feeling of it inside her was larger and more alive than the growing babies. More painful, too.

"Don't say that, Tom," she begged him in a whisper. "I love the way your family works. It's— You asked me this afternoon what I was afraid of losing, and that's one of the biggest things. I don't want to lose your family."

"But why would you? Only if—"

"If there's a divorce," she finished for him baldly.

"A divorce. Is that what you want?"

"No. *I* don't. I— Nothing's changed from what we agreed at the start. The babies still deserve our best effort." It was a stilted phrase.

"Yeah," he growled. "I wouldn't disagree with that."

He seemed disappointed with her answer. Which was a pity, since she'd only been telling him what she thought he wanted to hear.

The sexual tension between them was thicker than soup. Wasn't it? Tom asked himself doubt-fully. Or was it only coming from him, surrounding him, eating him up so that he was blinded to the fact that all Julie felt was—

What? What did she feel? She was sitting back with her hands folded beneath her rounded abdo-men, looking a million miles away.

But he'd been a man when he got up this morn-ing, and he wasn't going to turn into a mouse now.

You're not going to do this to me again, Julie, he thought. *You're not going to make me doubt my-self to this extent. I know you're hiding something, and if it's not that you don't want me, then it has to be that you do. All I still need to know is why.*

He dropped his fork onto the almost empty plate of bread cubes, slid from the low chair and moved to crouch beside her on the floor. Deliberately, he reached out and began to trace one finger lightly across the back of her hand, speaking softly at the same time.

"I remember a day two and a half months ago,"

he said. "The day after our wedding, when we both
wanted each other so bad that it hurt."

He let his finger climb higher, to her forearm,
and watched the fine, almost invisible hairs there
stand up to attention. She was watching, too. Saying
nothing. Not moving. Definitely not pulling away.
Her breathing was coming a little quicker.

"I remember," he went on, "that we actually
admitted it to each other, and laughed about it, but
that didn't make it go away. Probably made it
worse."

His finger reached the sleeve of her cherry pink
maternity top, and he traced the curve of her upper
arm then cut quickly up across the thick, soft fabric
to her neck and continued his teasing journey to
arrive at the sensitive skin beneath her earlobe.

"I remember some sadist, disguised as a doctor,
telling us we had to wait a week, which we managed to do—heaven knows how—and then at the
end of that week—only *just* at the end of it—I remember us aching so badly, needing each other so
badly, that we barely made it to the bedroom."

He leaned closer and replaced his finger with his
mouth, touching her skin softly, then tasting her,
sliding his kiss down her neck from her ear to her
collarbone, then toward her lips. His mouth was
warm and seductive, and he was acting like he'd be
happy to take all night over this.

She shuddered. "Tom…"

She turned her head to him, closing her eyes,
inviting his tender invasion of her mouth. She

wanted to lose herself in this forever. She wanted to let her bones melt and her brain turn to spun sugar.

But he wouldn't abandon himself fully yet. He had more to say. "And it was so good, Julie, wasn't it?" he whispered against her mouth. "I can't have been wrong about that."

"You weren't wrong," she admitted, parting her lips and darting her tongue against the corner of his mouth.

"It was fabulous. Earth-shattering. *Wasn't* it?"

"Yes. Yes, it was."

"But afterward, *immediately* afterward, that same day, you switched off like…like the New York State power grid failing. I mean it was *sudden,* Julie! And when I tried to talk to you about it, you just *wouldn't,* and when I tried to…well, seduce you, basically, you closed up on me, and I—"

He pulled away and spread his hands, declaring his helplessness, holding it out to her in his hands, *giving* it to her like it was something valuable and important—which, he was starting to realize, it was. Perhaps if he wanted anything to come out of this weekend, he had to start by admitting his helplessness over the issue of Julie and their marriage.

"Tell me what to do, Julie," he said, looking into her eyes and threading his fingers into her hair. "Tell me what I have to do to get you to tell me you want me."

"Do you need me to say it?" she asked. "It's obvious, isn't it?"

"Then why did you switch off?"

"Because I was scared that if we made love, I'd lose the babies."

"But Dr. Stern said—"

"I had another bleed. I—I didn't tell you. Not a bad one like the first time. But when I called Dr. Stern—"

"Where the hell was I while this was going on?"

"You'd gone out for milk and the newspaper."

"And you didn't *tell* me?" He rocked on his heels then stood and wheeled around to face the fire, standing so he could lean against the mantel.

Julie could see his anger. Could practically see the steam coming out of his ears.

"I didn't want to worry you." Part of the truth, anyway.

"Bull!"

"What, do you think I *did* want to?" She stormed to her feet. "That I was looking forward to you walking in the door again so I could tell you, 'Guess what, my body's having another go at losing them'?"

"No! Hell, Julie…"

"When it happened, when we slept together, it was so wonderful. To feel the weight of you, and the way you whispered my name. But I wanted more. I wanted it built on something rock solid, and I felt—I felt as if—" She stopped, distracted.

They were arguing about something that had taken place nearly three months ago. But this was here and now, and something strange was happening. It had happened about ten minutes ago, and she'd wondered about it. Not worried. Just wondered. Pregnancy brought with it so many odd feelings. If you took notice of every one of them, you'd be a wreck. And if you called your obstetrician every time, he'd have to put in extra phone lines.

This time the feeling was stronger. More distinct. A dull ache in her lower belly, building to the point of pain, in perfect unison with a tightening sensation, like scalp muscles tightening in fear. After about thirty seconds, it ebbed, leaving only the vague sensation of discomfort she'd had—if she really thought about it—ever since this afternoon's fall.

"What is it, Julie?"

"Nothing." She shook her head, still frowning, touching her abdomen lightly.

The word was far more about convincing herself than it was about fobbing Tom off, but he didn't see that, of course.

"Nothing?" he yelled. "Don't *give* me that, okay? I'm trying to get through to you and *still* you're trying to push me away. *It's not nothing.* It's enough to distract you totally from what we were in the middle of, and that means it's something we should share. So shoot! What *is* it?"

"I—I thought I felt some pain, that's all."

"Pain? You mean—?"

"I don't know, Tom." She was close to tears. "I've never done this before. Have you? An ache, okay? A tight feeling. It's gone now. Maybe it's normal. Maybe I'm still a bit shaky from that fall.''

''Has it been just the one time?''

''No. There was one about ten minutes ago. This one was more intense.''

''I don't like the sound of this.''

''And I don't like the feel of it,'' she admitted.

''Oh, Julie.''

He reached out for her, and they held each other. She felt the nudge and press of his chin as he kissed the top of her head, and wanted to bury her face in his neck and inhale the scent of him, utterly familiar and right with its mixture of soap and skin and salt.

''Sit down,'' he said after a few moments. ''Try to relax. Let's see if it comes again.''

It did. Ten minutes after the last time. Stronger. Longer. More intense.

Third time lucky? Tom kept telling her to relax, but he looked as tightly wound as a cat about to spring.

He called Dr. Stern while Julie was supposed to be lying on the couch, breathing deeply. She didn't for a second believe that breathing deeply would help and knew that her shallow, frightened panting didn't quite cut it, either.

''He says you're doing the right thing,'' Tom reported ten minutes later, after another regularly paced swell and ebb of sensation. ''Breathe and relax.''

''But I'm not! I can't!''

''We're to go straight to the ER at the nearest

hospital and get you checked out.'' He shoved his cell phone in his back pocket. ''I'll get our coats right away.''

They were on the dock before the next pain hit. The Sportsman was safely moored.

Tom didn't waste any time. He leaped into the boat and tossed a thick comforter over the hard bench seat so Julie could lie down. Then he reached for her, taking her weight fully in his strong arms as he swung her toward him.

He climbed to the black bulk of the outboard motor while Julie lay balanced on the narrow plank.

Tom wrenched at the pull starter of the motor, bracing his feet wide to get the best stance, making the boat rock. The motor sputtered into life, throbbed and swelled then coughed and choked and died.

''It's okay,'' Tom muttered automatically. Then swore.

He yanked at the starter again, tinkered with the controls, hissed as he plunged his arm down into the icy water to check that the propeller was free of weeds, then yanked the starter again.

The sputtering sound was lamer than ever. He tried one more time, and all he got now was a feeble growl.

''It's not going to start,'' he said heavily.

They both knew it.

Now that he'd stopped trying, the whole surface of the lake seemed utterly silent and ominously dark. Apart from the light fingering down from the windows of their house, only one summer home was lit, on the far shore, too far off for anyone to hear if Tom shouted.

He was watching the lighted windows all the same. "They've got a boat," he said. "I remember from the summer. They water-ski. There it is, that gray shadow, down by their private dock. If I knew their name, I could call them on the cell phone. All we need is their boat for ten minutes."

He eyed the black stretch of lake water, and Julie saw the calculation and intent in his eyes. He was getting ready to swim.

"You can't! Tom!" She grabbed his arm roughly, not caring if she hurt him.

"I'm a strong swimmer."

"It must be three-hundred yards."

"Five hundred," he corrected absently, still assessing the situation. "I could do it in ten minutes. Maybe less."

"...and it's freezing! Tom, even if you made the swim safely, you could die of hypothermia afterwards."

"This is my fault," he said grimly. "Don told me the Sportsman's motor was iffy. He wanted to check it out this afternoon. I wouldn't let him. I was too impatient. To be alone with you."

He was sitting down, reaching for the laces on his shoes. She got there first, gripping each double-knotted bow tightly in her fists, refusing to let him reach them. What he'd just said hardly registered. "You *will not* do this!"

He only stared at her stonily and said, "Okay, then I'll leave my shoes on."

"Call Don, for heaven's sake! You have the phone! He can come across in the other boat."

"He lives over half an hour away."

"I don't care!"

"You could lose the babies, Julie."

She was weeping, fighting to grip him, any part of him, while he was trying to shake her off. She was winning, but only because he didn't dare put any real strength into the fight for fear of hurting her.

"I'd rather lose the babies than lose you, Tom. Oh, I mean I know I'll lose you anyway, if I lose the twins. There'll be no reason for us to stay married. I owe Mom for pointing that out, when I first told her I was expecting twins and having trouble. But at least you'll still be *alive!* Call Don, Tom, if you care anything at all about what I feel." Her words ended in a desperate, jerky sob.

He didn't speak. Just reached into the back pocket of his jeans and pulled out the phone.

It took him just a few seconds to punch in the number, and after a short silence, he said in a voice of iron control, "Don? It's Tom. Can you get over here straight away and bring the Riviera out to the island? You were right about the motor on the Sportsman. It's dead. And we need to get to shore and into Glens Falls Hospital as soon as we can." A tiny pause, then, "Don't ask questions. There isn't time. Just come."

It was back in his jeans pocket a minute later. Then he knelt on the hard, wet fiberglass of the boat's bottom, wound his arms around Julie's shoulders, pressed his cold forehead against hers and said in a voice that left no room for doubt, "Now, tell me again what you said about losing me. And what does any of it have to do with your mother?"

They had plenty of time. They were both too scared for anything but honesty.

"I love you, Tom," she told him. "So much! And I've been so scared of losing what we had before it even truly began."

"Me, too," he growled. "I think it started the day we met, and by our wedding day I was already more than halfway there. But I'm a pretty smart guy, and I still can't figure out how loving me—oh, Julie, you don't know how good it feels to hear you say it—translates into holding me at arm's length, never touching me, avoiding me whenever you could. I started to think you didn't want our marriage at all. This weekend was my last stand. You know I don't take defeat lying down! So tell me!"

"Because I was so scared that if I admitted how much I wanted you, we'd sleep together again, and it might trigger a miscarriage.

"My mother made me see the cold, hard facts. I called her while you were asleep that day, thinking she'd be pleased to hear our news, and all she could tell me was that it was a pity I'd done it to you."

"Done it?"

"Saddled you with a pregnancy and the obligation of marriage. I told her I'd been having some
trouble, and she said if I lost the twins it would be
for the best. We could 'start over.' Split up, in other
words. And I knew she was right. Without the babies, our agreement meant nothing. We could start
divorce proceedings the next day. The whole reason
we came together, the bond between us, would be
gone. It was like being torn apart. I knew I loved
you, and yet to have any chance of keeping you in
my life, I had to push you away."

"Do you think I'd just have thrown you out if
we'd lost them?"

"Of course not. It wouldn't have been as clear-
cut as that. But back then, at the beginning, the
babies were the only thing that bound us. Without
them, I was so sure we'd just drift apart."

"I had the same fears," he said.

"And how could it have been different, when we
didn't know each other?"

"But it's not like that anymore, Julie," Tom
whispered. "You know that, don't you?"

"Oh yes, Tom, and—"

She stopped and gave a gasp as another contrac-
tion began to build. He gripped her hands then tried
to kiss her, and she lifted her face at the wrong
moment so their lips met clumsily. It didn't matter.
It still set her on fire.

"Getting stronger?" he asked.

She shook her head. "About the same. Maybe even a little weaker."

There was a silence. They didn't kid themselves that the apparent lessening was significant.

"Your hands are freezing," he said softly, bringing them to his mouth and blowing on them, then kissing them.

"I forgot to put on gloves."

He reached behind her and lifted the rest of the comforter across so that it blanketed them both, her lying down and him sitting there, crouched uncomfortably on his haunches.

As the pain ebbed, she said shakily, "If this labor can't be stopped, I really will lose them, Tom. I'm only twenty-two weeks. If they were born now, there's no chance they could survive."

"I know, my sweet darling, I know."

"I don't want it to happen! It's…it's *unfair!*" She gave a bitter laugh through her tears. "But it happens to people, doesn't it? We're not the first."

"But we're together," he whispered. "Whatever happens, good or bad, there's that, and it means we can get through this. I love you, Julie. Our marriage is real in every sense of the word. It's not the babies that bind us now, even if the worst happens. It's our love, and I'm *never* letting you go!"

"I'm going to hold you to that. Keep saying it. I love you, too…keep holding me now, please!"

He pulled her face against his shoulder, then their mouths met in a hungry kiss that said even more than the incoherent words that spilled from them both. Finally they were silent and still, just sitting, not daring to risk walking to the house, keeping each other warm, waiting.

Half an hour later, they heard the throb of the boat growing louder as Don gunned it across the black waters of Diamond Lake.

Epilogue

"Mom! How did you get here so quickly?" Julie said, struggling to sit up a little higher in her hospital bed.

She'd been on the point of falling into a doze, and she'd hardly recognized Sharon Gregory at first, so well concealed had she been behind an enormous arrangement of flowers in a cube-shaped china vase.

Sharon plunked the flowers down on the bedside table. A wash of thin January sunlight fell across them, making their warm colors glow against the backdrop of bland hospital walls.

"Thank that husband of yours," Sharon said, with a wry expression. "He's...uh...very forceful on the phone. I got a few home truths, Julie, and— Well, let's put it like this, will you forgive me if I admit I deserved them?'' The appeal in her face was very real.

"Of course I will, Mom," Julie answered huskily. Forgiveness was easy today.

"He reserved me a round-trip ticket, too—and paid for it. Which was wonderful of him, but I took the hint and I told him so.''

"Matt didn't come?"

"He's in the middle of shooting.''

"Not another faceless gangster role?'' Julie said without thinking. She felt pretty groggy and preoccupied over the twins, and had taken her mother's words too literally.

Sharon beamed. "No! The absolute opposite!'' she said. "Oh, Julie, it's just so great! I haven't wanted to distract you with our news since you've been having such a hard time yourself, but he's playing the lead in a great new feature. Low-budget. Independent studio. But the director is the hottest thing in town at the moment, since he won a huge award at Cannes last year, and the script is fabulous.''

"That's great, Mom!''

"Better yet, since word got out that Matt had the role, my phone's been literally hot with people calling for him. And I've got five new clients now, who were so impressed at the way I was handling Matt's career they wanted me to represent them as well. I got one of them a national commercial last week. It's going to make such a difference to us, honey!

Last year was hell! We were both on the point of giving up.''

"Oh, Mom…''

"Yes, it really had got to that point! I didn't want to tell you. Definitely didn't want to *face* you, when I knew you didn't want me to marry Matt in the first place.''

"No!''

"Honey, admit it. You had huge doubts. And I understand that. It was scary for me, too. But since the new year, things couldn't be better with his career, and even if Tom hadn't called to say you were in labor I'd have been on the first plane after I heard about the birth. Where are my gorgeous grand-daughters?''

"In the special care unit.'' Julie's throat tightened.

That awful and wonderful night at Diamond Lake had been only the beginning. She'd stayed in Glens Falls Hospital for several days, then transferred to Philadelphia's Pennsylvania Hospital. After nearly three months in the hospital to keep her persistent premature labor at bay, she had finally given birth last night, four weeks early, with Tom at her side throughout.

The two girls, each weighing just over five pounds, were normal and well-developed, but their breathing hadn't been quite right, and Julie couldn't relax. She'd lived with this fear about her babies for so long that it was starting to seem like a permanent part of her, a hard-edged little lump that lived somewhere between her throat and her chest.

If it hadn't been for Tom, talking her spirits up, aching with her, loving her...

Here he was.

As always, her heart turned over at the sight of him, dark and tall and smiling just for her.

"Hello, gorgeous," he said softly.

If he'd noticed there was another woman in the room, he wasn't letting it worry him. He came to the bed and reached for her hand, then kissed her long and slow. "Did I hear you saying something about Maggie and Rosie being in the special care nursery?" he asked finally.

"Yes, I was telling Mom." She nodded. "Mom, this is Tom, at last. Tom, my mother, Sharon Gregory."

"Hi."

They nodded at each other and shook hands. It was a little awkward.

But then Tom cocked his ear at the bumping sound of wheels in the doorway. "Guess what," he said. "They're not in the special care unit anymore. I've just come from there, and the pediatrician has given the okay for both of them to stay with you and go back to the regular nursery if you're tired. Here's the nurse bringing them now."

"She is? And they're really okay." Tears sprang into her eyes. "I can't believe it."

The next two hours were close to heaven.

Sharon was tearfully delighted with the two tiny,

black-haired girls. And Beth and Jim dropped in and met their son's mother-in-law as well as their new granddaughters.

"Nice to get you alone," Tom whispered, stretching out on Julie's bed as soon as they'd all gone.

"We're not alone," she pointed out. "We have Maggie and Rosie right there."

"They're asleep," he growled. "For the moment, they don't count."

It still didn't seem quite real. Didn't seem possible, after all they'd been through. By this time, half their married life had taken place right here at Pennsylvania Hospital, in a room just like this one.

Tom had come to see her every day, and when he hadn't been here, he'd been on the phone. They'd spent hours like that, as if they were teenagers not allowed out on a school night.

Getting their relationship back to front again.

Getting pregnant before they met. Hanging out on the phone after they got married. Falling in love before they knew all those little things people come to know about each other. Bonding over their babies before they even knew there were going to be two of them.

"I'm so proud of you," Tom said. The labor hadn't been long, but the pushing part had been. Two hours to birth Maggie and another half hour for Rosie. "And I love you so much. I can't wait to get you home. When will it be? Did Dr. Stern say?''

"Tomorrow. I thought I might have to go home without Maggie and Rosie, but now they'll be coming, too. Oh, Tom!''

"I really, really, really can't wait,'' he said, moving closer to her and gathering her into his arms.

"I know.''

"I have it all planned, you see. The very first thing we're going to do is tear up that prenup contract. We should have done it months ago.''

"We could have,'' she agreed. "But this way, it's a real celebration.''

"And the very second thing we're going to do is…''

He didn't bother to finish, but the deliberate, suggestive brush of his mouth across hers permitted no doubt about what he meant.

"Uh, Tom…''

"Yes, my darling?''

"I…uh…haven't told you *everything* Dr. Stern said this morning, have I?''

"Okay. Just give it to me straight. How long is it this time?'' He wore a suffering look.

"Six weeks,'' she whispered.

"Six weeks? I tell you, that man is trying to do himself out of business.''

"Well, you know, with two babies in the house we might actually find we don't have the energy for—''

"Stop, Julie,'' he growled. "Let's both stop

while we're still ahead. All I can say is that if I didn't have your beautiful mind and your beautiful heart and your beautiful children to distract me, the coming six weeks would probably be the longest ones of my life.''

"But once those six weeks are up, I'm thinking about a couple of the things we'll do right now," she said innocently, and grinned as he swivelled away from her, groaned and buried his face in his hands.

*   *   *   *   *

MILLS & BOON®

Makes any time special™

Mills & Boon publish 29 new titles every month. Select from...

Modern Romance™   Tender Romance™

Sensual Romance™

Medical Romance™   Historical Romance™

MAT2

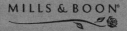

4 FREE

books and a surprise gift!

We would like to take this opportunity to thank you for reading this Mills & Boon® book by offering you the chance to take FOUR more specially selected titles from the Modern Romance™ series absolutely FREE! We're also making this offer to introduce you to the benefits of the Reader Service™—

- ★ FREE home delivery
- ★ FREE gifts and competitions
- ★ FREE monthly Newsletter
- ★ Exclusive Reader Service discounts
- ★ Books available before they're in the shops

Accepting these FREE books and gift places you under no obligation to buy, you may cancel at any time, even after receiving your free shipment. Simply complete your details below and return the entire page to the address below. *You don't even need a stamp!*

YES! Please send me 4 free Modern Romance books and a surprise gift. I understand that unless you hear from me, I will receive 6 superb new titles every month for just £2.40 each, postage and packing free. I am under no obligation to purchase any books and may cancel my subscription at any time. The free books and gift will be mine to keep in any case.

P0ZEA

Ms/Mrs/Miss/Mr ....Initials....................................
BLOCK CAPITALS PLEASE

Surname ....

Address ....

....

....Postcode................................

Send this whole page to:
UK: FREEPOST CN81, Croydon, CR9 3WZ
EIRE: PO Box 4546, Kilcock, County Kildare (stamp required)